AF613669

Fred M. White

The Mystery of Room 75
(Murder Mystery Classic)

e-artnow 2020

Fred M. White

The Mystery of Room 75 (Murder Mystery Classic)

Crime Thriller

e-artnow, 2020
Contact: info@e-artnow.org

ISBN 978-80-273-3656-2

Contents

I - THE "AGONY" COLUMN

Wendover was feeling just a little good-natured contempt for himself. He would not have cared to admit that he had been following the girl down the Strand, but it was more or less the fact, though he had not the least intention of speaking to her, or molesting her in any way. Paul Wendover was a University man, and a gentleman, and he had the healthiest contempt for the class of cad who does that sort of thing.

He was following the slim figure with the tinge of titian red in her hair in the direction of Fleet-street out of a spirit of mingled curiosity and admiration-that intangible something where woman is concerned that always moves man, sooner or later, even though he happens to be a busy journalist, with his whole soul wrapped up in his profession. Wendover would have indignantly denied that he had fallen head over ears in love with a stranger whose features he had not even seen, except a fleeting glance at a perfect little profile, the vision of a slim and slender figure, and a mass of hair that seemed to have caught the sunshine and retained it.

And so Wendover wandered on, keeping the girl in sight on the off-chance, perhaps, of meeting some casual acquaintance who knew her. He had heard of such things, and fortune is always on the side of those seekers after adventure who pursue her steadily. Moreover, it was a case where Satan finds some mischief still, for idle hands to do, because Paul was taking more or less of a holiday after a long spell of strenuous work on the Continent, where he had been investigating certain anarchists' haunts on behalf of his paper, 'The Daily Herald.' He spoke half a dozen languages fluently, he was skilled in various disguises, and he asked for nothing better than to take his life in his hands occasionally, whenever there was danger to be found. In short, he was the star man on the 'Herald,' a brilliant descriptive writer, and an athlete to his finger tips. He had just wound up a successful investigation and he was back in Fleet-street now, with the intention of dropping into the 'Herald' office presently to report himself, and, like a journalistic Oliver Twist, ask for more.

And then, as he strolled along, the dazzling vision with the red-gold hair had drifted across his path, and, on the idle impulse of the moment, he was following her, though he would have found it difficult to explain why. He was interested, he was more interested still when the girl suddenly started and swerved across the pavement away from a thick-set man with a big felt hat pulled down over his eyes. Evidently the girl was startled, and, perhaps, not a little afraid, for she would have passed on hurriedly if the somewhat forbidding-looking individual had not detained her.

"Ah, this is an unexpected pleasure," he said, in a foreign accent that was irritatingly familiar to Wendover, though he could not for the life of him recollect where he had heard it before. "You haf forgotten me, Miss-er—"

Paul could not catch the name. He was standing near enough, under the pretence of gazing into a shop window, to catch snatches of conversation. He heard the girl whisper a name under her breath, then she would have hurried on again but the man prevented her. Wendover's fingers clenched, and the blood began to sing in his ears.

"I am in a hurry," the girl said.

"So! I should not have thought so by the way you were sauntering along. But why are you angry with me, Zena? This little trouble of yours is no fault of mine. It was not I who suggested that your father, before he died, should give everything to the Brotherhood. And perhaps I can help you, even now, if you will let me. If it is a question of money—"

"You know it is," the girl whispered passionately. "You know that I have nothing except what I can earn. You know that during my father's last illness his mind was utterly gone. Otherwise he would never have left me penniless, except for what I can earn as a dress designer."

"I am sorry," the man said. "But come this way and let us talk it over. Let us turn into a cafe and have some tea. It is not for my health to stand here, for I know not who is watching me. Come along."

The girl hesitated for a moment, and then followed her companion through the doorway of the teashop. Wendover followed in his turn, but the place was more or less crowded, so that he had to take his place at a table a little away from the others. From where he sat he could only hear a word here and there, catch a question now and again, and its muttered reply. He heard allusions to the Ambassadors' Hotel, that famous cavaranserai in Piccadilly, and something in connection with a dance that was being given there by the Associated Arts Club. Then there was a further rush of customers, and Wendover could hear no more. He waited a little time, but the two sitting at the table opposite did not seem disposed to move; then, with an impatient sigh, he told himself that he was a curious fool, and went more or less reluctantly on his way towards the offices of 'The Daily Herald.'

The Editor of the 'Herald' was in, and would be very pleased to see Mr. Wendover at once. The great man shook hands with his contributor, then closed the door of the office carefully and gave orders down the telephone that he was not to be disturbed. He took from his desk a scrap of paper.

"I was very pleased with those last articles of yours," Sutton Deane said. "They were great. But weren't you just a little reticent?"

"I had to be, my boy," Wendover explained. "As a matter of fact, I haven't finished yet. It was no very difficult matter to lay that poisonous scoundrel, John Garcia, by the heels and see him safely shut up in Geneva. But I could only do it on a trivial charge, and, in the ordinary course of events, one of the most traitorous scoundrels in Europe will be free again in a few months, unless I can find the additional evidence that I am now looking for. That fellow is the head of a very dangerous gang; he is as false to his friends as he is to his foes, and the world will be well rid of him if I can get my proofs before he is released from prison in Geneva. That is why I am over here, more or less taking a holiday and making inquiries. You see, there's plenty of time. And if I can do what I think I can, then the 'Herald' will have the biggest scoop in the history of the paper."

"Yes, that sounds good," Sutton Deane said thoughtfully, "but are you quite sure you have laid John Garcia by the heels?"

"Of course I have. I put the police in Geneva on his track, and he was arrested a few days later. Gorzia, of the Swiss Intelligence Department, told me so, and subsequently I read that Garcia had had six months for some trivial offence-travelling without a passport or something of that sort. But why?"

"Well, look at this. It is just a scrap of paper, as you know, merely an advertisement from our 'Agony' column of last Monday. That is the original copy handed in downstairs with five shillings for its insertion. Now, you know how interested I am in criminals and their ways. If any advertisement out of the common comes in, I always ask for it to be brought up to me, so this scrap of paper came my way in the usual course. Read it."

Wendover read the scrap of paper as follows: —

"Brotherhood. Ambassadors' Hotel, Friday. Don't forget the Associated Arts Club Dance."

There was no more than that, but it touched Wendover's memory. It struck him as just a little strange that the mysterious couple he had been watching in the tea-shop had mentioned both the Ambassadors' Hotel and the Associated Arts Club Ball. That keen journalistic nose of his began to scent out a paying mystery.

"Well?" he asked. "And what does it mean? I might tell you something about it myself, but I am not going to do so for the moment. What I am after just now is information. You didn't refuse that advertisement, I hope. Don't tell me that the 'Herald' has suddenly become squeamish. It is no doubt a signal from one set of thieves to another, but if you become particular about that kind of thing you won't get much revenue out of your agony column in the future."

"Ah, that's not quite the point," Sutton Deane said. "I don't know why, but this particular advertisement aroused my curiosity, so I told the people downstairs to hold it back, and if the man who brought it in came to complain, as he was pretty certain to do, the people behind the counter were to pretend to make enquiries and apologise, and send for me, so I could look at the chap. When he came next day, and kicked up a fuss, just as I expected, I had my chance to look at him. Of course the advertisement went in next day, but I gained my point, and had seen the man who brought it in."

"Well, I hope it was worth all the trouble."

"It was, my boy, it was," Sutton Deane said. "Now I am going to startle you. Do you remember when we were in Paris two years ago you pointed out to me in the Cafe de l'Europe a man who, you said, was the biggest scoundrel on the western continent. And you mentioned his name?"

"I remember, it was John Garcia."

"Just so. Well, the man who brought that advertisement was John Garcia. There is no mistaking the chap when once you have seen him, and you know my extraordinary memory for faces."

"But, my dear fellow, it is impossible!"

"Impossible or not, I am sure I am not mistaken. Now, don't you suppose that the police possibly might have blundered? May not they have in their their custody another fellow who is acting the part of chief conspirator, so that the leader himself might be free to knock about Europe, when all the police are under the impression that he is safe."

Wendover was silent for a moment; for once in his life he was utterly taken by surprise. Such tidings had happened before, and they might quite reasonably happen again.

"Well," he said presently, "it may be so. On the other hand, you may have been deceived. Now, look here, suppose I take this matter up. I presume there will be no difficulty whatever in getting me a ticket for this Art Club dance?"

"You mean to go?" the editor asked, eagerly.

"Most assuredly I do," Paul said. "I want to go for more reasons than one. And, unless I am greatly mistaken, I am on the verge of the biggest adventure of my life."

II - THE GIRL IN RED

It was shortly before eleven o'clock on the evening of the Associated Arts Club ball that Paul Wendover turned into the Ambassadors' Hotel. It was a beautiful June evening, peaceful and placid, and, outwardly, at any rate, there was no sign of coming strife or trouble. In its way the Associated Arts Club dance was an important social function, though the great hotel, with its fine suites of rooms and the most competent staff in Europe, made little or nothing of it. Half-a-dozen big dances had taken place there without disturbing the thousand or so of guests who passed every night under that magnificent roof in Piccadilly.

Paul Wendover looked, in his six-feet of splendid manhood and immaculate evening dress, a typical, well-groomed Englishman, who was out for an evening of simple pleasure. He strolled through the reception rooms towards the ballroom with the air of a man who has nothing on his mind, and who is bent entirely on looking for casual acquaintances. And certainly, in the ordinary way, the Associated Arts Club dance promised to be amusing. To begin with, it was emphatically a Bohemian function of the most brilliant kind, and everybody connected with literature and the stage would probably be present. Just for a moment Wendover stood there, regarding the ebb and flow of beautifully-dressed women and well-known men, and then he thrilled and stiffened to his fingertips as his eye encountered a slim figure in scarlet-the figure of a tall, graceful girl, brilliantly fair and dazzling, her head crowned with great masses of orange-red hair, twisted like a coronet about her brows.

It was the girl that Wendover had seen in Fleet-street that afternoon. He knew that he could not possibly be mistaken. And yet there was nothing about her now to suggest a girl who is struggling to keep her head above the social waters. She seemed to stand out from the rest of the crowd like a thing apart. It wasn't altogether that she was more outstandingly beautiful than many other exquisitely-dressed women there, but there was about her some intangible charm and distinction that seemed to lift her, in Wendover's eyes at least, far and away above the rest of them.

To begin with, it seemed to him that she looked as no Englishwoman could have done. And she was all the more attractive because the man she was with was not in the least distinguished. He was just an ordinary Englishman, sandy-haired and freckled, a man with whom, as a matter of fact, he had been at school.

But Wendover had no eyes just then for Sir Peter Cavendish; he was looking at the girl to the exclusion of everything else. She seemed to float round the room with the nameless grace and abandon of a beautiful scarlet butterfly. And, against the deep red of her dress, and the dazzling whiteness of her arms and neck, that marvellous hair of hers stood out like a dart of flame. Then, presently, the music ceased, and the girl and her partner went back to their seats. Wendover saw his acquaintance rise presently, and wander away in the direction of the smoking-room. He stopped just for a moment as Wendover accosted him.

"Who is the Lady in Scarlet?" he asked, carelessly. "Not English, I feel sure."

"Oh, no," Cavendish replied. "French, I think. Very attractive, but not quite my style. I was introduced to her by Vera Bentley, of the Frivolity, so, of course, I had to ask her for a dance. Like a good many other striking looking girls, she is dull, with little to say for herself."

Wendover elevated his eyebrows sardonically. Cavendish was by no means intellectual, and his limits were bounded by horses and golf clubs. Wendover knew he was mistaken. He could read a fine intelligence and a beautiful intellect in that lovely face and those dark, liquid eyes. Still, it was futile to argue the matter out with a man like Cavendish.

"You surprise me," he said. "But one never can tell. By the way, what is the lady's name?"

"Zena Corroda, the daughter of the scientific johnny who made lots of money out of scientific experiments. One of those birds who are born to put the world right. Down on chaps with money, and all that. They say that the old cove was a bit of an anarchist in his way."

Wendover started slightly. He was on the track of the mystery now, for the things that Cavendish spoke of vaguely were part of a big, open book to him. He was seeing his way more or less clearly into the heart of things. He made some excuse for shaking his loquacious acquaintance off, and made his way back into the ballroom. As a matter of fact, he was more startled and uneasily interested than he was prepared to admit. For he wanted to help the girl with the red hair, the girl who stood on the threshold of a great danger. The spirit of adventure was in his blood now, but he had something to think of besides the interests of his paper.

He was going through it all now, as he stood there nodding and smiling to passing acquaintances, but with his mind far away. He was uneasy and disturbed too, as he always was till he had got hold of the right thread, and then he would plunge into the heart of the danger with a tranquil mind and an utter disregard for his own safety.

And that the girl was in some bitter trouble he felt certain. She was seated all alone now, an utter stranger in that brilliant, frivolous, dazzling crowd, a thing apart from all the rest, and almost pathetically lonely. She sat there for some time, utterly unconscious of the fact that she was being watched, and perhaps forgetful that she was there at all, and then she looked up presently, and, like a flash, the settled melancholy in her eyes changed to abject terror.

She half started from her seat, then dropped back into it again, with pallid cheeks and parted lips, and with her hand pressed to her heart, as if some mortal pain were there. It was only for a second or two, and then she recovered herself.

But, in that instant it seemed to Wendover that he had discovered the source of the trouble. He could see a tall, thin man, clean shaven and hawk-looking, making his way round the ballroom in the direction of one of the palm-lined corridors, where a series of dimly-lighted alcoves had been arranged for the use of such of the guests as wanted to sit out a dance or two. And no sooner had the man with the hawk-like face and sinister eyes vanished down the corridor than the girl rose as if impelled by some force, and followed him.

A minute later Wendover followed in his turn. He had no excuse for doing this, he told himself; it was sheer impertinent curiosity on his part, but he rose and went. It was just at the beginning of the corridor that he overtook the girl.

"Excuse me," he said, "but may I speak to you for a moment; Are you not Miss Zena Corroda?"

The girl turned a startled face upon him.

"Oh, yes," she said, "but please do not detain me. There is someone, a gentleman, who has just gone along here, that I want to speak to at once. I have a message for him which must not be delayed."

"You think he is in danger then?" Wendover asked coolly.

"Oh, yes, yes. But how do you know that? Who are you that dares to stop me in this fashion?"

"I am your friend, I think," Paul said quietly. "In fact I know I am. Don't think me presumptuous, but I am sure you are in trouble, and I want to help you. Have you ever heard your father speak of Mr. Paul Wendover?"

"The name seems familiar," the girl said. "I think there was a journalist of that name—"

"Yes, that's right," Wendover said eagerly, "I am the man. I came on behalf of my paper to interview your father in Berlin. You would probably have been a girl at school at that time. And now, Miss Corroda—"

The girl looked about her like some beautiful, hunted creature, who seeks an avenue of escape.

"Oh, please don't keep me, please," she implored. "God knows I want a friend, for I am all alone in the world, and I feel you are sincere in what you say, for you look like an English gentleman. If you have anything more to say, will you please stay here for two or three minutes, and I will come back to you. But, please let me go now."

Wendover drew back with a muttered apology. So far it seemed to him that he was gaining ground, and, at any rate, the girl had promised to return. He waited there, in the empty corridor for the best part of ten minutes, waited there quite alone, till he began to grow anxious and uneasy, and then, moved by some impulse that he made no effort to restrain, he strolled down the corridor, turning his eager gaze into the various little palm-lined alcoves, most of which were empty with the lights turned on. It was as quiet and solitary there as if it had been miles from Piccadilly, and no sound to break the silence but the distant murmur of the band.

There, at the far end of the corridor, in one of the tiny retreats, dimly lighted by a solitary lamp, it seemed to Wendover that he could see a smudge of scarlet with a suggestion of dazzling white here and there, bending over some blurred object that lay hidden behind a clump of ferns. There was something so sinister about the whole thing that Wendover rushed in and stood there, with startled eyes.

For there, behind that screen of greenery, lay the dead body of a man in evening dress. He lay there with his eyes turned upwards, lay there with a cruel gash in the centre of his dazzling expanse of shirt front, on which the crimson stain stood out vividly. And standing over him, frozen with horror, was the girl in the red dress.

"You cannot believe it," she whispered. "You cannot believe that I—I—"

"Of course not," Wendover said. "Such a thought is impossible. But you know who the man is?"

"Yes. It's Detmar-Leo Detmar. The man I came here to warn all too late."

From the distance came the dreamy music of the band, and between those two and the dim alcove lay the body of the murdered man. Wendover was the first to recover himself.

"I must get you away from this," he whispered.

III - "A FRIEND IN NEED"

A glorious gratitude swam into Zena's eyes.

"Then you are going to help me?" she whispered.

"Of course I am," replied Wendover. "What could the average man do less? I find you here in bitter distress, and there is nothing else for me to do. Oh, you need not look at me like that. Do you suppose, for a moment, that I can associate you with a deed of violence that has resulted in the death of the man who lies there? Of course not. No one in his senses could. But then you know who he is."

The girl seemed to hesitate for a moment, not that there was any sign of hesitation or confusion about her. She was terribly moved and shaken in every limb, but, withal, she displayed a quiet courage that compelled Wendover's admiration. And then the incongruity of the scene forced itself upon him. At any moment they might be discovered by some passing reveller, at any moment some loving couple might intrude upon their privacy. And then, of course, awkward questions might be asked, and the beautiful woman in the red dress find herself in a position of deadly peril.

Wendover already knew that she had not a friend in the world, knew that she depended upon her personal endeavours for her daily bread. And yet, here she was in this exclusive gathering, beautifully dressed and looking as if she and poverty had never even been nodding acquaintances. No doubt she would be able to explain presently, for Wendover was sufficiently a man of the world not to judge by outward appearances.

"You must come away," he said hurriedly. "You must come with me back to the ballroom, anywhere away from here, for it seems to me that it would spoil everything now if a lot of awkward questions were asked, and, besides, you have nothing whatever to do with this crime. Come with me, and let us go away from it as far as possible."

They stepped out into the corridor side by side, and Wendover noted with a sigh of relief that the place was as quiet and deserted still as it had been a quarter of an hour before. It was quite evident to him that no one had seen Zena Corroda enter the alcove, and his movements had been unmarked by anyone. He drew the girl's shaking arm through his, and led her back to the lights and the music, and the chatter of the frivolous crowd with a feeling that all this was a dream, and that he would wake from it presently.

Sooner or later the body lying in the alcove would be discovered, but that was no reason why he or she should be identified with it. Indeed, such a course would go a long way to hinder him, and thwart the discovery of the crime and rascality that he was already tracking down. And the girl appealed to him. That wondrous and pathetic beauty of hers touched him as he had never been touched before. He was more than half in love with Zena Corroda already, without knowing it.

He seated her in the quietest corner of the ballroom he could find, and insisted that she should take a glass of champagne. He watched the color creeping back into the olive-tinted cheeks, and the frightened, haunted fear dying out of those dark eyes of hers.

"You are indeed a friend," she whispered.

"Until death," Wendover said, with a tinge of passion in his voice. "I want you to believe that there is nothing in the world I would not do for you. And perhaps a little later on you may like to confide in me."

"Then you implicitly trust me?" Zena asked.

"Absolutely and implicitly," Wendover said. "Still, this is a serious business, and I have more than an impression that you know something about it. I am more than certain that you do. When the man who lies dead yonder passed you just now in the ballroom, I was watching you. I have been watching you more or less, all the afternoon. I saw you in Fleet-street. I saw that man stop you, and I followed you into the tea shop. Don't ask me why, Miss Corroda, because I cannot tell you. I really don't know. Why does a man who takes only a general interest in women suddenly find himself arrested by a face in the crowd? Why does a man find himself irresistibly attracted towards a woman he has never spoken to? But these problems can wait. When the dead man passed you you turned pale, and your eyes were full of trouble. Then you followed him, to warn him, probably."

"Oh, I did," Zena said. "The man was in great danger, how great a peril you have seen for yourself. More than that I cannot tell you at present."

"Oh, I think you can. I think you must. And there was another man, too, who followed directly afterwards, another man who went down the corridor, and who either turned into one of those alcoves or into one of the rooms at the end of the corridor. Did you see him?"

"No," Zena explained, "but I know that he must have been there. It was against him that I went to warn the man who is dead. And the other man, who was responsible for the crime, no doubt, disappeared in the way you have suggested. And now, Mr. Wendover, I am going to tell you something. Because you are my friend, and because my heart tells me that I can trust you. Beyond that locked door at the end of the corridor lies the whole secret. Beyond that door is the fortune that my father made, and which would have been mine had he been left to himself. When I came here to-night, partly with the intention of enjoying myself, I had forgotten for the moment, that the Brotherhood meets in this hotel once a year to discuss the future, after supping together. It was my father who founded the Brotherhood, and all that remains of them now are John Garcia, Leon de Vince, Nikolo Petroff, and Leo Detmar, the man who lies in the corridor there, stabbed to the heart, and two others whose names I forget. As I told you just now it had escaped my recollection for the moment that the Brotherhood meet to hold their annual supper and conference in this hotel. You must understand that my father has been dead over a year now, and these people, for the most part, ignore my existence. It is quite clear to me that Detmar was lured here and murdered in that alcove by one of his own colleagues—"

"Murdered by John Garcia, you mean," Wendover suggested.

Once more the look of terror crept into the girl's eyes.

"What do you know of him?" she whispered.

Wendover waved the suggestion aside. There came back to his mind the recollection of what Sutton Deane had told him and the mysterious advertisement in the 'Agony' column of the 'Herald.' it was quite clear to his mind now that some strange mistake had been made by the police, and that John Garcia was at large. Moreover, he had lured his victim here and had murdered him with matchless audacity in the midst of the dance. It was a crime worthy of the man called John Garcia.

"It matters little for the moment what I know about him," Wendover said; "the question is-where is he now."

"In room 75," Zena said. "He had a latchkey to that room, and so have the others."

"But why should he destroy his friend?"

"Why does that type of man always commit a crime?" Zena demanded. "For money, of course. These people call themselves patriots, they profess to wage war on capitalists, but what they all want is their share of the hundred thousand pounds which form the funds of the Brotherhood. And those funds are locked in that safe, in room No. 75. Some day all but one of those men will be dead, or hanged, and the survivor will be rich beyond his wildest dreams. My father was a visionary and an enthusiast, and the dupe of these men. That's why he left all his money to the Brotherhood, and why I am compelled to earn my daily bread. Oh, if I only had someone bold and resolute to help me!"

"You have," Wendover cried. "I will help you. I will do anything to help you, and all the more so because I myself am on the track of those scoundrels. I have been shadowing them for months. But this is a phase of their rascality that I had not contemplated. You see, Miss Corroda, I am a journalist, attached to the 'Daily Herald,' and adventure is the breath of life to me. It is incidental, perhaps, but there is no occasion for me to work for my daily bread, though I love the life for its own sake. And I am going to help you, because I want to, and because I want to rid the world of these poisonous scoundrels, and, if I can help you in the meantime, it would only add zest to my success. Now, perhaps, you will honor me with your confidence."

Zena smiled gratefully into Wendover's eyes as she produced from the folds of her dress a black silk mask, edged with gold filigree, and the half of a broken circular gold disc stamped with the figure 3. The gold disc had been broken across the centre, so that only half of it remained. And these things the girl handed over to the puzzled Wendover.

At the same time there was a third object that Zena laid on Wendover's palm, which, for the moment he had overlooked—a small latchkey, apparently of the Yale pattern, though a little longer in the wards than is usually the case. But, for the moment, this did not hold the same fascination as the broken gold disc, with its section of a figure 3. Apparently the disc had been fractured across the middle, as if some strong hand had bent it backwards and forwards until it was broken.

"Don't you think you had better begin at the beginning and tell me the whole story over," he suggested. "At present these mysterious objects convey nothing to me. All I can see is that by great good fortune I can help you in more ways than one. As I told you just now, I have been tracking this infamous Brotherhood half over Europe during the last six months on behalf of my paper, and now I am going to track them on your behalf as well. I am going to lay them by the heels, and I am going to recover for you the money which is justly yours, and of which you have been robbed. Mind you, I am no child at the game. I am a strong man, with a love of adventure, and I am alive to all the cunning and chicanery of these cosmopolitan scoundrels. And, whatever happens, I am always and ever your friend."

Zena's dark eyes were full of gratitude.

"Then, my friend, I will tell you," she whispered. "There is not much time, but I will do my best."

She bent towards Wendover, till he could catch the subtle fragrance of her, and the elusive perfume of her hair. There was entire trust and confidence in those luminous eyes of hers, a confidence that touched Wendover and stirred him as he had never been stirred before. He half inclined towards her, with an air of protection that she, in her loneliness, found infinitely sweet and soothing.

"You are very, very good to me," she murmured, "to me, a stranger. I wonder why?"

"Because you are young and beautiful and lonely," Wendover whispered passionately. "Because I am a man, and you appeal to me for protection. And most of all, perhaps, because you are you. Zena, do you know how lovely you are?"

The red blood flamed into the girl's cheeks.

"I wonder if you know how good you are to me," she said. "Oh, thank God. I have at last found a friend."

"Go on," Wendover said. "Go on."

"Well, it's like this. You have met my father, and you must know that he was both a scientist and a dreamer. More by good fortune than anything else he made a good deal of money over an invention of his. Then he got caught up in that dreadful Brotherhood. It was indeed an evil day for him when he first came under the influence of John Garcia. I always mistrusted that man myself. I hated that bald head and strong, oily face of his. I hated his manner, and the furtive way he looked at one. But he talked well, and he posed as the friend of mankind, and the inveterate foe of the oppressor in all walks of life. And that is how the war between the Brotherhood and the Big Trusts began. It was with my father's money that that last corner in wheat was broken. But I am sure that Garcia was always a traitor."

"Always," Wendover said, "but go on."

"He was one of the few men amongst the Brotherhood that I knew by sight. The rest of them had assumed names, and whenever they meet, they are always masked. There came a time when my father realised all his money and converted it into notes and gold. That money was placed in the safe in this hotel, and locked, by means of a time lock, which only opens automatically at a certain moment, once a year. No one else could open it, because, when once the combination has been arranged, the safe must remain secure for a given period, and that period is midnight of this very day, in every June. The room itself is always locked, and has a limited number of keys, one of which is in the hands of each of the Brotherhood. And that is one of the keys I have just given you. Once a year, the council meets here, to discuss its policy for the coming twelve months. On these occasions they allot certain funds for certain purposes, and these are distributed amongst various members of the council. But, roughly speaking, there is a hundred thousand pounds in the safe, but where it will be after midnight when the strong room opens automatically I cannot say. It may be all gone."

"At any rate, it is safe for the moment," Wendover suggested. "Now, I was under the impression that the man called John Garcia was safely locked up in Geneva. Things have happened during the last few hours that make me feel that I am not justified in that belief. I think now that Garcia managed to substitute someone for himself, and, that being so, he is enjoying a freedom from police supervision that he has not known for years. It was I who got him locked up, and I hoped, before he came out again, that I should be able to lay before the authorities such information as would lead to the scoundrel being hanged. But, apparently, he has baffled me, and eluded the police at the same time."

"Have you ever met the man?" Zena asked.

"Only once," Wendover explained, "and then in a bad light. I understand he is wonderful at disguises, but I think if I heard him speak I should know him again. By the way, what is the fellow really like!"

"He is short and stout and red of face, and he has not a hair on his head," Zena explained. "Once seen he can never be mistaken. But, surely, you are wrong in saying that the man is still in gaol, because, as a matter of fact, John Garcia was with me in the tea shop this afternoon."

"Really," Wendover exclaimed. "Now, you know, I took particular note of that man. So far as I know I have never seen him before, though his voice struck me as being familiar. When I was spying on you this afternoon I caught the sound of the words that he said, and I knew that I had heard that voice before. I was worried, because I could not couple it with any particular individual. But it did not matter much, except that forewarned is forearmed. With this knowledge I shall be still more useful to you."

"Then you are going on?" Zena asked. "You are not afraid, even of John Garcia."

"Without boasting, I don't think I'm afraid of any man," Wendover said. "My dear Zena, there is nothing I wouldn't do for you. It seems to me that, as you have placed in my hands the means of getting inside that chamber and attending a meeting of the Brotherhood, I should be a poor sort of creature if I did not avail myself of it. I have taken greater risks than that. Oh, I shall be safe enough. They would never dare to lay violent hands upon me, under the roof of the Ambassadors' Hotel."

But Zena was not listening. She was watching a man in evening dress, making his way through the crowd in the direction of the corridor. She gripped Wendover by the arm.

"Look," she whispered, "there is Garcia himself."

"You are quite sure of that?" Wendover asked.

"Oh, I cannot be mistaken, I know the man so well. That is John Garcia, beyond a doubt. He must have escaped from prison, as you suggested, or he has cleverly contrived for the police to arrest somebody else."

"I begin to see it," Wendover said. "It becomes as plain as daylight to me. By some means or another Garcia discovered his danger, and induced that unfortunate Leo Detmar to impersonate him. Then, when Garcia was safely out of Switzerland, Detmar obtained his release. He was on his way here to-night to attend the meeting of the Brotherhood, and was, no doubt, foully murdered in the alcove by the very man whom he had served so well. He was lured into the alcove by means of an advertisement in the 'Agony' column of my own paper. I only found that out by accident this afternoon. Then, after the crime was committed, Garcia hid himself in the locked council chamber for a few moments, and now he has come out again for some purpose of his own. Yes, the more I think of it, the more sure I am of my facts. Detmar is out of the way now, his disappearance will convey nothing to the rest of the Brotherhood, and Garcia will be here to-night, masked and unrecognisable, and probably tell the Brotherhood that he is representing Garcia, and that the latter is still in gaol. You can see for yourself how this course will help that murderous scoundrel to get all that money into his own hands."

"How wonderfully clever you are," Zena said. "But you may never leave that council chamber alive. You see, that room belongs to these people. They pay a big rent for it, and it cannot be used by anybody else. The door fastens with a patent lock, and there are only so many keys, all of which are in the hands of the Brotherhood. I believe the manager of the hotel has one, but it is merely so that the room can be cleaned out from time to time, and a supper laid once a year. It is a cold supper they have, a luxurious meal with the choicest wines, but no waiters are present. The hotel people regard the Brotherhood as a set of eccentric millionaires, who meet once a year to celebrate some particular occasion, and, as they pay well, always in advance, no questions are asked."

"Oh, I quite understand that," Wendover said. "London is the only place in the world where people can do those kind of things. But never mind that. You have given me all I need; but what about these identity discs! I suppose the other halves are somewhere."

"In the safe," Zena explained. "A measure of precaution. If anybody tries to get into the council chamber with a forged disc, it will be compared with the other half, and if the ragged edges do not fit, the imposter would be detected at once. Do you know that I took those things you have from Detmar's dead body in the vain hope that I might find some friend to use them for me. I tremble to think how I could have done it."

"It was a brave thing to do," Wendover said. "And now, for your dear sake—"

Zena held out her hands impulsively. The tears were trembling on her lashes now, like twin diamonds, her whole heart was in her face.

"Dear little girl," Wendover whispered, "wish me good luck. It only wants a few minutes to midnight, and I must be up and doing. Now, take your courage in both hands, and behave as if nothing had happened. I suppose you have at least one friend here to-night."

"Just one," Zena replied, "the actress friend who lent me this dress, and who is here somewhere."

"Very well then, seek her out, make her find you a partner or two, try and behave as if you had nothing on your mind. I will be back as soon as I can."

As Wendover spoke, a big clock in the neighbourhood struck the hour of midnight. He jumped hastily to his feet, and strode away in the direction of the corridor, leaving Zena seated there, a prey to a thousand fears.

But, from that moment, Wendover had resolutely put her out of his mind. With his courage strung to the highest pitch he pushed his way along till he came to room No. 75.

The well-oiled lock gave instantly to the key, and a moment later, after he had donned his mask, and felt the gold disc safely in his pocket, he passed through an ante-room, into the council chamber itself.

As he did so, the big marble clock on the mantelpiece struck twelve. The great adventure had commenced.

V - THE TIME LOCK

Wendover glanced about him casually. His first care was to convey the impression that this was by no means the first time that he had been present in the Council Chamber.

He saw a large, well-lighted room, elaborately and artistically furnished, in the centre of which was an oval table set out with supper for apparently half a dozen people. It was an extravagant cold repast, and on a sideboard in one corner of the room stood a number of bottles capped with gold foil. To the left of the draped and curtained window was a writing table, and over this, let into the wall, the door of a safe that swung open, as if pulled back by unseen hands, at the very instant that the clock on the mantelpiece finished striking twelve. There was something almost uncanny, almost forbidding in that quiet movement.

There were five men in the room besides Wendover, each of them wearing a similar gold-fringed mask to the one that covered the daring adventurer's face. No one took the slightest notice of him, no one bowed as he took his place, indeed, it seemed as if his intrusion had been more or less expected. He was face to face now, and well he knew it, with a handful of the most desperate criminals in Europe, each of which would have slit his throat without the slightest hesitation if only he made one false step. But he knew that his credentials were good, he had the gold disc in his pocket, and his mask was in perfect order. Then, cautiously, but with an air of careless indifference, he began to take stock of his companions. He saw a little man, with a dark olive complexion and closely trimmed beard, and yet another one, tall and swarthy, and spare to leanness. There were two others, one slender, yet wiry looking, with hair of a peculiar flaming red, with a touch of orange in it, and the last man short and thickset with a hideous twist in his lower lip, that a seemed to throb as if it had a pulse in it. These were details which Wendover's trained eye and instinct absorbed and noticed almost mechanically. He knew, only too well, that these little signs and portents would interest him later on.

But it was the fifth man who attracted Wendover's particular attention—a man short, and inclined to be fat, and absolutely bald, with clean shaven lips which were thick and sensual, and hard and cruel at the same time. A blunt, pugnacious nose was scarcely concealed by the mask behind which Wendover could discern a pair of eyes, dull and lifeless, and at the same time menacing as those of a snake. The mask disguise was enough for all practical purposes, but those dreadful lips were not lost upon Wendover, and he knew now that he would recognise the man before him whenever they met in the future, and under all conditions. And that his very existence depended upon this remembrance. Wendover knew as if the man had risen from his seat and had threatened him by name. He knew that here was the man John Garcia, the man whom he had truly believed to be a prisoner in Geneva. But that had been all a mistake of course. In the light of recent information, gained only a few yards away there in the ball-room, Wendover had learnt, by a piece of pure good fortune, that his plans had miscarried. Doubtless John Garcia had obtained early tidings of his danger, and, secure in the knowledge that he was not known by sight to the Geneva police, had cajoled the hapless Detmar into impersonating him for the moment.

The confirmation of this inspired Wendover, and spurred him on to the effort that lay before him. He had a healthy respect for this chief foe of his, and, indeed, for every man who sat round the table. For they were all after one thing. They called themselves anarchists, and the foe of the oppressor in every land, but every one of them, seated there, behind his black mask, turned a restless glance every now and again in the direction of the open safe. It was the contents of the safe they were after. For the sake of its precious contents, they were prepared to commit any crime under the sun, and they were prepared to sacrifice one another, and all the time John Garcia was sitting there, with murder in his heart, deliberately planning the destruction of his colleagues. One by one he would strike them down, as he had struck Detmar down an hour or so ago, with an unparalleled audacity that stamped him as a master criminal. And it was amongst those that Wendover had come, taking his life in his hands, fighting for a great stake in a good cause, for a pure and beautiful girl and the fortune that was undoubtedly hers.

And, even as he stood there, conscious of his danger, he had his dreams. He knew that he had challenged the powers of darkness for something more than pure chivalry. He was stretching out his strong, right arm for the lifelong happiness and prosperity both of Zena Corroda and himself. And it was characteristic of the man that he had already made up his mind as to the future. It would be no fault of his if he did not win something infinitely more precious than the tempting vein of wealth behind that open door.

It was John Garcia who spoke first, though, naturally, he did not speak in his private capacity, nor, indeed, were the Brotherhood aware of the real identity of the individual who addressed them. This was the reason for the masks—a precaution against treachery from one man to another. Garcia spoke in a hard, rasping voice, not much above a whisper, that carried to the farthest corner of the room.

"I am here with a message," he said. "I come here, representing the man who is known to you all by name as John Garcia, our accredited leader. So far, no one has seen him in the flesh, at least, under his proper name, and only about two of you, if as many, have the privilege of knowing him. Now, Garcia has been betrayed into the hands of our enemies by someone outside the Brotherhood. Just for the moment it matters nothing who it is who has been guilty of this thing. Garcia will know, in due course, how to punish the author of this black treachery."

A murmur of approval ran all round the room.

"Sufficient for the moment it is that your great leader lies in a foreign gaol," the speaker went on impressively. "But not for long, not for long. And, once he is free, he will know when and where to strike. Let it be assumed that I am here, acting on his behalf. Believe me, my friends, when I tell you that the proofs of this black treachery on the part of one that your leader never harmed, lie within the sealed envelope that I hold in my hand."

Wendover held his breath for a moment. There was an unexpected development that he had not anticipated. What if his secret had been disclosed, what if the president of the Brotherhood knew that the man who had been tracking him down sat there, helpless and unarmed, within a yard of vengeance? And if this was so, then the great adventure was over, almost before it had begun. And yet it seemed impossible that Garcia should know, indeed, how could he, when the gold disc and the mask had only passed into Wendover's possession half-an-hour ago? He bent over the table with assumed indifference, yet with every muscle tense and rigid, and with every fibre of his being ready for the fray.

"Open it," the man with the orange hair said. The President shook his head, and, as he did so, Wendover knew that the crisis was passed.

"Not to-night," the leader replied. "That is not the wish of the man whom we regard as our head. My instructions are that this envelope should be deposited in the safe, behind those locked doors, for another twelve months."

Wendover was breathing freely now, he breathed more freely still as he saw Garcia place the envelope in the safe.

"Come, comrades," he said, "let us go through the form of proving our right to be here."

So saying, he took from his pocket the section of his own gold disc, and the other men immediately followed his example. Wendover's precious fragment lay on the table, almost as soon as the rest. No sooner were they displayed than, from the interior of the safe, Garcia produced their corresponding halves. Then he lifted the discs, one by one, and gravely proceeded to fit them to the sections that he had taken from the safe, so that, presently, what appeared to be six complete coins lay before him. This being done, he handed back to each man his token of identity with the air of one who is thoroughly satisfied with his task.

"Before I close the safe for another year," he said, "before I set the combination which bars that lock for another twelve months, in such a way that it cannot open in the meantime, I wish to ask the usual questions. Is there any member of the Brotherhood present who is in need of funds to complete the peculiar task upon which he is engaged? We have one or two big operations in progress, and it may be that all of you are fettered by the need of money."

"I am, for one," the tall man with the black moustache said. "I need a thousand pounds. That strike in the Westphalian coalfields has not been quite as successful as I anticipated, and further funds are needed."

"Is it your wish, brothers," Garcia asked, "that our friend should have this money? Nikolo Petroff, I think."

The tall man bowed gravely. No hands were upraised in opposition, and the money and notes were handed over to the tall man, who placed them in his pocket. Then another, who was spoken of as Leon de Vince, proffered a suggestion, and he, in his turn, was duly accommodated. Wendover made a careful note of these names for future use. Then, nothing more being asked for, the leader commenced to arrange the numbers on the lock. A moment later the door of the safe would be closed again and, for a further twelve months, the treasure lying there would be safe from further depredations. But in twelve months much can happen. If fortune were on his side, Wendover might return a year hence, and restore the money to its rightful owner. As he thought of this, his spirit rose.

As if on the spur of the moment. Garcia turned to Paul and spoke. There was a sneer in his voice, and a glitter in his eyes, a hard and cruel gleam.

"Have you no request to make?" he demanded. "Is your particular task going so well that you have no occasion to make a call upon our common fund?"

VI - DANGEROUS GROUND

"I have no occasion to complain," Wendover said coldly. "I am thinking of the daughter of the man who founded the League, who, I understand, is left absolutely penniless. I propose, sir, that you seek this girl out, and hand her at least 500. It is only fair."

As Wendover spoke he saw, at a glance, that this proposal did not commend itself to the Brotherhood, though it seemed to him that the man with the orange-colored hair nodded approval, and the man with the twisted mouth smiled.

"Perhaps you know the lady?" Garcia sneered. "Perhaps you would like to convey the money to her yourself."

"I should," Wendover said coolly. "In a way, I do know her, and I am aware of her dire need. I will put it to the vote, if necessary."

The man who posed as Detmar hesitated for a moment. Then he produced a packet from the safe, and threw it contemptuously across the table in Paul's direction.

"Better count if for yourself," he muttered.

A moment later Wendover nodded, and a second after that the safe door crashed to with a bang, locked and barred, and impervious, except to the hand of an expert, and for the next twelve months. Paul knew that the fortune was safe. At any rate, twelve long precious months lay before him.

Without another word Garcia moved in the direction of the supper table, and there, under the rays of the electric light, followed the most remarkable spectacle that Paul had ever witnessed during the whole of his connexion with the 'Daily Herald.' It was strange to sit there gazing at those other masks, to sit there in absolute silence, and no word was spoken till the repast was finished, and the last bottle of choice champagne stood empty upon the table. Then the conversation became more general, though it was entirely restricted to commonplace discussions, as if each man mistrusted his colleague, and feared to say too much.

But it was not time lost, so far as Wendover was concerned. With that trained journalistic eye of his, he was taking in every little peculiarity and mannerism of his companions. He knew, at any rate, the names to which they answered, and the names by which, no doubt, they were known to the world generally, and that he would see most of them again, Paul did not doubt.

He had them all labelled and catalogued presently in his brain, and now he was more or less free to let his mind wander. Ever and again, from time to time, the sounds of mirth and laughter in the ballroom, and the strains of the band penetrated beyond the locked door, but not one of the men seated round the table appeared to heed it, or to be struck by the contrast between themselves and the mirth and gaiety going on within a few yards of where they were seated. The clock on the mantelpiece struck the hour of one before Garcia suddenly rose and advanced towards the door.

"Good-night, comrades," he cried, "and au revoir till this day twelve months. Great events will happen in that time, and may your efforts be crowned with success. I go first, as usual, and you follow, one by one, at intervals of two minutes, so that no man sees the other's mask removed. It is this precaution that shields us against treachery."

With these words Garcia vanished, and the outer door closed suddenly behind him. With one eye on the clock, Paul waited till the two minutes had elapsed, then he arose before any one could anticipate him, and, bowing to the other men, departed in his turn. He was prepared to run any risk and any hazard now to keep Garcia in sight. It was in his favour, too, that he was clad in evening dress, so that, once outside, with his mask removed, he could mingle with the mob of guests assembled for the dance, and follow his quarry unnoticed. He had not seen Garcia without his mask, of course, but he had made a perfect mental impression of that short, stout figure, and that bald head, and, given any luck, he would be able to follow up the trail and mark his man down.

He was in time to see Garcia turning out of the corridor into the ballroom, and, before the latter had reached the foot of the staircase, and had entered the vestibule of the hotel, Paul was close behind him. Just by the office a waiter stopped Garcia and gave him a message. The latter frowned and shook his head. Paul was near enough now to hear what passed between them.

"Tell the gentleman it is impossible that I should see him at this time of night," Garcia said. "Say that I am tired and am just going to bed. If he will call to-morrow morning at ten o'clock I will see him with pleasure."

The waiter came back presently, and, after a word or two with Garcia, went off in the direction of the smoking-room. Paul marked the waiter down for future use, and then made his way back towards the ballroom.

He was keeping his ears open now, alert and vigorous to know if anything unusual had happened during the last hour. But, apparently, there had been no gruesome discovery, and, apparently, the body of the dead man still lay in the alcove, where, possibly, it might remain concealed for a day or two. For the dance was still at its height, and there was no sign of alarm or disturbance or hesitation anywhere. Beyond doubt, things were just as they had been when Paul turned his back upon the ballroom an hour ago. Still, it ought to be all right, and if, at any moment, a waiter, or a couple in search of solitude, blundered on the body of Detmar, then it would be impossible now to connect Zena Corroda with that ghastly business. And, for the moment, Wendover was not thinking about it at all, for he could see nothing just then but the white, despairing face of Zena, looking out at him, like a head of death, behind a mask of gaiety. It seemed as if she were stretching hands to him across the ballroom, much as if he had been a rope flung to her across a stormy sea. He crossed swiftly to her side, and furtively pressed the hand that she held out to him.

"Courage," he whispered, "courage. You see that I have come back safely to you, and, so far, all is well. And I may tell you at once that I have not been wasting my time. So far my mission has been highly successful. But please-please don't look at me like that."

"Am I attracting attention?" Zena asked, anxiously.

"Well, apparently you are not," Paul smiled. "It is hardly your fault. I suppose these people here are enjoying themselves so much that they have entirely failed to notice that white, despairing face of yours."

"Is it so very noticeable, then?"

"Well, yes. And yet I gather that nothing has happened. The gruesome discovery has not been made?"

"It couldn't have been," Zena said, "or I should have heard something about it. I am sorry to think that you should consider me such a coward, but the waiting has been dreadful."

Paul smiled down into the white, anxious face.

"Poor little girl," he said tenderly. "I can quite understand how your nerves have been tried. But what have you been doing? Where is your friend?"

"I think she has gone," Zena explained. "At any rate, I have not seen her for some time now, and, on the whole, I think I have been happier by myself. Now, do tell me what you have done. Tell me in as few words as possible, because I am longing to get away."

"A little more courage," Paul whispered, "and then I will see you home. I have made pretty sure of my ground, but in a big thing like this, where the risks are so great, one must not neglect even trifles. I must have a word or two with a certain waiter here before I leave."

A little sigh escaped Zena's lips.

"I am quite in your hands," she whispered, "you know that I trust you implicitly."

Wendover looked down into the beautiful eyes, with a world of passion in his own, and pressed the slim fingers again.

"And you shall never regret it," he said. "I am your friend for life, and to help you is my own thought. No, don't thank me. It is pure selfishness on my part, because, dear child, you are so beautiful, and I never met a girl before who appeals to me as you do. But don't let us forget the practical side of things, Look at these."

As Paul spoke, he took the packet of bank notes from his pocket and laid them in the girl's lap. Then, in a few words, he explained how they had come into his possession. He caught Zena's sigh of gratitude, and saw the tears in the eyes that she raised with more than thankfulness to his.

"Ah," she said, "if you only knew what it meant to me. It is not so much the money I am thinking of, as of the knowledge that, for the moment, my future is provided for. It is only a lonely girl like myself, struggling hard in cold-hearted London for a bare living, who knows what it is to be without a shilling. But there, what about yourself? Are you in any danger, Paul?"

"I should say that we're all in danger," Wendover said, coolly. "And I more than suspect that that rascal, Garcia, is aware of what he owes me. Still, I'll never rest till I have dragged the last sovereign from that rascal's clutches. His scheme is to destroy us one by one, so that he can return to that room, in a year's time, alone, and possess himself of your fortune. It will be my wits against his, my clean hands and the strength of body God has given me, against black deceit and cunning. But I shall win, Zena, and when I do, I will come back to you, and ask for my reward. One moment, there is the waiter I spoke about."

Paul crossed to the man and slipped a coin in his hand.

"Who is that gentleman with the bald head you were speaking to just now?" he asked.

"That, sir," the waiter said. "Oh, a great Hungarian millionaire, who frequently stays in the hotel. His name, sir, is Mr. Leo Detmar."

So far, so good. It was all plain and clear now. Wendover crossed the ballroom and gave Zena his hand.

"Come along," he said, "your patience has been rewarded now. I have found out all I wanted, and now I am going to see you home. It seems to me that I shall have a very busy time before me during the next few months."

VII - ALONE IN LONDON

So far so good. Nothing could have fallen out better. For the present, at any rate, Wendover had marked his quarry down, and in all probability he would have a day or two in which to mark out a definite programme. Garcia appeared to be a fixture in the hotel for the moment, and this was all in Paul's favor. He was feeling slightly dizzy, and there was a vibrant humming in his head when he made his way down the stairs. It was as if he had been drinking too much strong wine. The contrast, too, from that mysterious room with those masked figures to the brilliantly-lighted ball room, gay with laughter and glittering jewels, was almost too much, even for his splendid nerve. But he was not dwelling upon that now: his one aim was to get Zena away without further delay, before the inevitable discovery of the body of Leo Detmar must be made. And so far there had been no disclosure of that ghastly crime. Otherwise things would not have been going on in the way they were moving at present.

Here was Zena, at length, seated safely in a corner of the taxi with a strained and anxious look in her eyes. She had done her best to forget the events of the past hour or so; she had had a dance or two, but she was beginning to wilt now, under the nervous strain, as Wendover realised directly he saw the purple shadows under those dark eyes of hers.

"So far all has been well?" he asked, eagerly.

"Nothing has happened so far," Zena whispered, "but you cannot tell how glad I am to be free again. A few minutes longer and I must have broken down. I had been dancing, as you suggested, but I could not get that dreadful alcove out of my mind. Up to a few minutes ago everybody has been dancing and supping, but my fear was that the trouble might appear at any moment."

The last words sounded almost like despair. Paul looked down at the girl with infinite pity in his eyes.

"You have been wonderfully brave and patient," he said, "and you are not going to be tried any longer. I am going to take you home. I shall never lose sight of you again, you dear, brave little girl. Your fine pluck would put courage into a coward—"

"If you only knew!" Zena whispered. "If you only knew!"

Ten minutes later the taxi pulled up in front of one of the smaller houses in Malden-street. Regent-street, a semi-private house, evidently devoted to a high-class dressmaker's business, for there was a foreign name over the front door and a large window on one side, in front of which the blinds were drawn.

"This is where I live," Zena explained. "I have a tiny bed-sitting-room on the top floor. Sometimes I work for the owner of the shop, but generally for myself. Madame Marbly is very kind to me; you see, she knows something of my story, and that is why I have a room for nothing."

"Do you live here all alone?" Paul cried.

"Oh, yes. There is no one here at present, except myself. But I do not mind, for I have got used to it. And there is a little sitting-room downstairs with a gas stove that I use in the winter time when I want to read. I'm not at all frightened. Will you-will you-come inside for a moment?"

Zena hesitated as she made the suggestion.

"I'm afraid I must," Paul said. "There is a good deal I have to tell you, and the sooner the better."

Zena switched on the lights in the little sitting-room, and dropped, tired and almost helpless, in a chair. Her beauty and loneliness appealed to Wendover with a new force. It seemed to him as if fate had designedly thrown himself and this girl together. In his case opportunity and inclination were hurrying forward hand-in-hand.

"I cannot tell you," he said, "how I admired your courage to-night. It is the courage that leads to victory. You and I together are going to win, Zena."

It seemed such a natural thing to call her by her Christian name, and the girl's pale face flushed with pleasure. She sat there, with her hands folded in her lap, listening intently to Wendover as he told his story.

"I always hated that man," she said. "But I did not deem that he was so black a scoundrel. He must be diabolically clever, too, to murder Detmar in this fashion and pass himself off as the dead man. Do you think that he means to serve the others in the same way?"

"I am absolutely convinced of it. The whole scheme is plain to my eyes. Garcia means to get the others out of the way, and time is on his side. Don't forget that he has a whole year in which to do it."

A startled look came into Zena's eyes.

"And you?" she asked. "What if he suspected you? What if he has found out that you are the man who betrayed him to the Swiss police? In that case is not your danger as great as the rest. If so, why go on!"

"There is that risk, of course," Wendover said coolly, "and the proofs are locked up in the safe. Mind you, when I got on Garcia's track I had no knowledge of the amazing romance into which I have blundered to-night. I only knew Garcia as a scoundrel and an international spy who is ready and willing to betray his comrades and his employers alike. And that is why I dropped a hint to the authorities. Of course he may have followed me to England; he may have recognised me to-night and decided to keep silent with a view to getting me out of the way in the course of time. But I am forewarned. It is his wits against mine. And I'll beat him yet. For the moment we need not discuss him any longer."

"But we must," Zena cried. "I cannot allow you to run into a danger like this for the sake of a stranger like myself."

"A stranger!" Wendover exclaimed. "Oh, Zena, don't call me that! There is nothing I would not do for you. And there's nothing you can say that will turn me back now. And I think the others are sorry for you."

"So you said just now. But what do you think of them? Are they sincere? Or do you think that, like Garcia, their one idea is to get hold of the money?"

"Oh, what does it matter? I tell you those men are doomed. They are mere puppets in the hands of a master conspirator. And I am bound to confess that I did not like what I saw of any of them. They belong to the wrong breed; in any case, we need not waste any sympathy on them. I am going to find out all about Garcia to-morrow, to discover whence he comes and how long he is staying at the Ambassadors' Hotel. And then I will have him carefully watched. I have only to drop a hint of what I have in my mind to the editor of my paper to have a free hand and spend as much money as I like in keeping Garcia under observation. And I must see you again. Suppose you meet me on Tuesday afternoon at half-past four in Kensington Gardens, and then we can have tea together and discuss the future. And whatever happens I am your devoted friend. I will never lose sight of you again, Zena, until this dreadful wrong is righted. And I will not leave you then unless you tell me to go. Never in my life—"

Paul paused and checked himself with an effort. Zena seemed to read what was passing through his mind, for she took his two hands impulsively in hers, and gazed at him with her whole soul, in her dark, unfathomable eyes.

"Good night," she whispered, "good night, and thank you from the bottom of my heart. Good night, my more than friend, for I trust you wholly and implicitly."

She lifted her eyes to his as she spoke, and he read something there in them that moved him strangely. He half bent down, and, at the same moment, with an impulse like that of a child, she raised her lips to his. It was all so sweetly and naturally done, so spontaneous, that there was not a touch of coquetry about it. It was very much as if a tired child was kissing some dear friend good night. And, in that moment, something passed between them, something strong, and yet intangible, that was destined to alter the current of both their lives. With the pressure of those lips still sweet on his, Paul went along the lonely street, absolutely deserted now, with his thoughts in a strange whirl.

For the moment, at any rate, he had forgotten entirely all about that thrilling adventure in the mysterious room, for his thoughts were more in the future than the present. He was with Zena alone; they were together in a world of their own, so that Wendover was barely conscious of the fact that he was treading the stony pavements of the West End. He became aware, presently, that someone was speaking to him, some foreigner in ragged attire, who was asking alms.

It was very lonely there, in that hour of the morning, for it was just 2 o'clock, and no policeman was in sight. Not that Paul was in the least alarmed, he was accustomed to be out at all hours, and he knew how to take care of himself.

"What do you want?" he demanded. "What are you doing here at this time?"

"I have no money; I am desperate," the man said.

"Well, I wouldn't be desperate if I were you," Paul said coolly. "It is a dangerous thing to be desperate in a London street at this hour of the morning. And I can assure you, my friend, I am quite capable of taking care of myself."

"I did not mean that, senor," the stranger muttered. "I am desperate that I have to beg for alms. Give me a shilling of your money that I can get a bed in this strange city."

Paul handed over the desired coin, at the same time eyeing the beggar closely. There was something about the man that did not suggest that he was in want, though he thanked Paul profusely, and turned in the opposite direction. Then he came back, creeping along behind his benefactor, and hiding himself in the shadows, so that Wendover smiled.

"So I am being followed," he told himself. "I am being tracked by some tool of Garcia's; it may be by the miscreant himself. Well, it is good of him to give me this warning, because it puts me on my guard, and more than ever convinces me that Garcia knew more than I gave him credit for."

VIII - FIFTY POUNDS IN CASH

It was quite late the following morning before Paul rose and breakfasted leisurely in his sitting-room. He had a small town flat, not far from the British Museum, where he had gathered together some of the treasures that he had collected in all parts of the world during his travels, for he was a born collector, and, moreover, quite apart from the income that he earned as a journalist, he had ample means to gratify his tastes. Therefore, the cosy little flat, under the shadow of the museum, was a perfect treasure house of trophies, earned by flood and field.

Paul ate his breakfast tranquilly enough, with a feeling in his mind that all was going well.

He had found, at length, the girl that he had been unconsciously looking for all these years; he knew that he had made no mistake, and that Zena was the one woman for him. He sat there, presently, smoking his cigarette, going over the events of the previous evening, and idly sketching out his plans for the future. Then the little heap of morning papers neatly folded on the table caught his eye.

"By Jove," he exclaimed, "I had almost forgotten that. I wonder if they have made any discovery at the Ambassadors' Hotel yet. They must have done so as soon as the guests had cleared out. I wonder if the 'Herald' had time to pick up anything for the later London edition."

Yes, there it was, with appropriate headlines. Paul read as follows: —

STARTLING DISCOVERY AT THE
AMBASSADORS' HOTEL.

Shortly before 3 o'clock this morning one of the waiters at the Ambassadors' Hotel made a gruesome discovery in one of the furnished alcoves leading out of the corridor of the suite of rooms that was occupied last night by the Associated Arts Club, who were giving their annual dance. In this alcove was the body of a well-dressed man, apparently about fifty-five years of age, lying there half concealed by a bank of ferns. The man, who was evidently a foreigner, had been stabbed to the heart by some sharp-pointed instrument, which had penetrated his dress shirt, which was stained with blood. From hasty inquiries made, it appears that the stranger could not possibly have been one of the guests, and a careful search of the body disclosed no sign of identity. Beyond a leather purse, containing three or four sovereigns, there was nothing to lead to identity, for the unfortunate man's linen was not marked, and was evidently purchased somewhere abroad. It is an undoubted case of murder, for the circumstances in which the body was found preclude any suggestion of suicide. The police are very reticent about the matter, and up to the time of going to press have absolutely declined to make any statement. The inquest will be held on Monday at 10 o'clock.

So, apparently, the police had made no discovery likely to lead to an arrest, and so far they had no clue to the identity of the dead body, for nothing was found in his pockets, and his linen and underclothing, which were obviously new, bore no identification mark. Nor, so far as Wendover could gather, was the crime associated in any way with the dance at the Ambassadors' Hotel. But though Wendover made it his business to inquire at Scotland Yard, he could not find that any discovery had been made in connection with the mysterious millionaires' club that had its headquarters at the great hotel in question. Obviously, then, it had not occurred to the hotel officials to mention the fact that a mysterious body of men had supped in the hotel on the night of the crime.

All of which was to the good, as far as Wendover was concerned, for he certainly did not want any inquiry into the meeting of the Brotherhood at that particular moment. He had ascertained definitely that Garcia had no intention of leaving London at present, and, moreover, that Garcia frequently occupied a suite of rooms at the Ambassadors', where he was an honored guest and spent his money freely. There had therefore been no difficulty in detailing a clever private inquiry agent and one or two assistants to keep a close eye on the sham millionaire. It was easy enough for Wendover to tell his assistants that he was doing this on behalf of the 'Daily Herald,' and make an excuse to the effect that Garcia was acting as the agent for a big international loan, and that the 'Herald' was interested in getting at the facts before the scheme was made public.

With all this off his mind Wendover met Zena on Tuesday afternoon in Kensington Gardens. She appeared to be eagerly awaiting his coming. She was dressed in a simple frock of white muslin and an inexpensive straw hat. But that was nothing that could detract from that marvellous beauty of hers, nothing that could rob her of that exquisite sweetness and the glory of her dark eyes.

She seemed eager and restless and somewhat excited as she placed her hand in Wendover's.

"You are punctual," he said, "and I think that you have some news for me. Am I not right, Zena?"

"Oh, yes," the girl cried. "A most singular thing has happened. I had a letter by the middle day post, enclosing me 50 in postal orders. I left those at my lodgings, of course, but I have brought the letter for you to read. Shall we sit down for a moment? There's a quiet seat here."

There were only two or three lines in the letter that Zena handed to her companion. There was no address upon it, and no signature save the sign, 'No. 4,' which was placed in inverted commas. With a knit brow Wendover read as follows: —

Dear Madam,

It matters nothing who I am, though you may make a guess as to whence I came and what the business of my life is. I heard, on Friday night, that your late father, in his zeal for the Brotherhood, had left you penniless. It will be my endeavour one of these days to try and right the wrong which has been done to you. Meanwhile I enclose you 50 in postal orders, which you may accept without loss of your proper pride and with the assurance that it is part of your own money.

"It is easy to guess where this came from," Wendover cried. "It was sent you by the tall man who was inclined to support me the other night when I advanced your claims. And that being so, you need have no hesitation in keeping the money, for it certainly came out of the safe. I suppose that fellow's conscience troubled him or he would not have done this, knowing you already had had 500. But that is not the point. I am particularly anxious not to lose sight of any of those men, but unfortunately I had to concentrate my attention upon Garcia, and that is how they escaped me. Now did you happen to look at the post office stamp on those orders? If you can tell me this it will not be long before I can locate the man who calls himself Leon de Vince. You see it is not a usual thing to send so large a sum of money in postal orders, and if they happen to have been purchased at a sub-office the girl behind the counter would be sure to have noticed him. If you will let me know—"

"I can let you know now. By chance I happened to notice the post office stamp. It was Church-street, Hampstead."

"What a splendid piece of luck!" Wendover cried. "I live in Church-road, Hampstead, as you know, and the post office in question is just round the corner. It is a little fancy shop, and the girl behind the counter is quite a friend of mine. This is going to help me materially. Now come along and have some tea and let us try to forget our troubles for the moment."

It was late the following afternoon before Wendover found time to drop in at the little post office at Hampstead and make his enquiries. He knew the audacious little blonde behind the counter, for he bought papers and magazines there, and he had never found the girl averse to a mild flirtation. Besides, he was a past-master in that kind of thing, and before long he had discovered that at the far end of Church Grove an Italian gentleman was lodging who rejoiced in the romantic name of Leon de Vince. It was good to know that the man was not disguised under a pseudonym. Moreover, Mr. de Vince was an artist of some repute in his own country, who had taken rooms in Hampstead with a view to finding a studio there. It was quite evident, too, that the romantic foreigner had made a considerable impression upon the empty-headed little shop assistant, for she seemed to know a good deal about him and his movements. She knew, for instance, that he was in the habit of going to town every night to some place of amusement or another, and that he was extremely fastidious as to his food. He had told her himself that very morning that there was only one place in London where a gentleman of taste could obtain a dinner worthy of the name, and that was at the Cafe Montagne in Regent Street, and that, moreover, he dined nowhere else.

Wendover knew that place by repute, a more or less fashionable cafe, well patronized by the better-class of foreigners and such Englishmen as have travelled largely. It was about five minutes to eight the same evening, therefore, that Wendover dropped into a seat in the Cafe Montagne in such a position that he could command the entire room, and waited for his man. It was about a quarter of an hour later that the tall Italian, with the drooping black moustache, followed on and took a seat which had evidently been reserved for him a few tables away. Despite the fact that the man had been masked when they had last met, Wendover had no difficulty in recognising him.

Immediately opposite, at another table facing the Italian, was an elderly clergyman, with white hair and long, luxuriant beard, staring about him like one who is for the first time in strange and uncongenial surroundings. As he opened his lips to give an order, Paul thrilled as he recognised the hard, cruel mouth of Garcia himself. Then Wendover sat back in his chair to watch the progress of events.

An hour passed, the diners were nearly through before de Vince half rose from his seat, and with a loud cry pressed his hand to his left side over the region of his heart. Then he collapsed over the table, and Wendover could see the red blood dripping drop by drop on the white tablecloth.

Wendover sat up, every nerve alert and quivering. His first impulse was to rush forward to the table over which de Vince had collapsed, but he restrained himself and remained where he was, watching everything from under his knitted eyebrows, and at the same time preserving an attitude of utter ignorance as to the tragedy which had taken place under his eyes.

He was cool and collected again now, and fully conscious of the folly of giving himself away. He felt, rather than knew, that the man with the grey beard and benevolent air, seated at the table fronting the one occupied by de Vince, was none other than Garcia, in an effective disguise. Did Garcia know that Wendover was watching him? Did he know of Wendover's identity, and that he was seated with in a few yards of the man who had betrayed him to the Swiss police?

This was the eternal danger that Wendover had ever to guard against. If yonder cold-blooded and calculating scoundrel was fully cognisant of these things, then Wendover's life was as much in danger as that of the unfortunate de Vince. It was madness to take risks now, so Wendover sat there quietly, and watched the progress of events from his table. Problems of this kind had become part and portion of his daily life. He had learnt to value even the smallest clue, and he was not going to forget his lesson at that moment. To begin with, he could see from where he was sitting that, from Garcia's chair, he had a clear and uninterrupted view of his victim, whom he was facing, and from whom he was separated by not more than four yards. This was the first point. The second point was that in front of Garcia, between the two small shaded lamps, was a vase of magnificent red chrysanthemums. One of these had fallen on the table, or rather had been broken off, for the head of one of the blooms lay on the white table cloth like a splash of blood. Apparently it had been severed from its stem at the base of the flower as if it had been cut off by a knife. Garcia himself sat as if utterly ignorant of the trouble; he appeared to have his table napkin bunched up in his right hand as if he had just been applying it to his lips.

By this time a group of waiters had gathered round the stricken man, and someone was calling aloud for a doctor. Almost instantly the whole restaurant was in confusion, and the wildest rumors were afloat. It was only a few minutes, however, before de Vince was carried away, and the restaurant began to simmer down again into something like order. Still Wendover never moved. Out of the corner of his eyes presently he could see that Garcia was paying his bill, and a little later on his table was empty. It was time to move now. Wendover called a waiter to his side, and began to ask questions.

"What was the matter with that unfortunate gentleman?" he asked. "It looked to me as if he had broken a blood vessel."

"'A most mysterious affair, sir," the waiter replied. "The gentleman was shot in the left breast. He was not badly injured, and indeed, the bullet had not penetrated far. But the doctor said if it had been inch the other way it would have been fatal. But he will get better, oh, yes."

"How did it happen?" Wendover asked.

The waiter shrugged his shoulders eloquently.

"A mystery, sir," he said. "No one saw the shot fired-in fact nobody heard it. It was as if an unseen man with an unseen weapon had done it. Of all the things that have ever happened here this is the most mysterious. Everybody is puzzled. Perhaps the gentleman himself can tell us something when he is in a state to talk. Meanwhile a doctor, who is one of our regular customers, has taken him away to Hampstead in a taxi. The police will see to the rest."

So far as it went this information was satisfactory enough. The one man who could throw some light on the mystery, beyond the victim himself, walked thoughtfully out of the restaurant presently, and himself took a taxi to Hampstead. He was very thoughtful as he drove along, but by the time he had finished his second cigarette he began to see a little light shining behind the veil of darkness.

He began to understand, too, what an amazing and audacious antagonist he had in the shape of John Garcia. Evidently the man would stop at nothing. Of his courage there could be no question. And doubtless he had thought this thing out to the minutest detail. He had made up his mind beyond question to remove de Vince and Nikolo Petroff as coolly and deliberately as he had made away with the unfortunate Leo Detmar. No doubt he had calculated on the fact that only two men who really mattered, in addition to Detmar, stood between him and the contents of that fire-proof safe, and therefore to a certain extent the unexpected appearance of Wendover, in the guise of one of the Brotherhood, had apparently interfered with his deep-laid plans. But whether or not Garcia could put his finger on Wendover as one of the persons to be removed was not troubling Paul very much at that moment. It was necessary, of course, to assume that such was the case, but just now there were more pressing matters.

For the moment, at any rate, the attempt on de Vince's life had failed. Not that this would prevent Garcia trying again and again, but not in the same way if Wendover could prevent it. And how had the thing been done?

By the time that Paul was comfortably seated in his own lodgings it seemed to him that he had solved that part of the mystery. And the clue of the broken chrysanthemum lying on that little table had been the key to the puzzle. With matchless and unparalleled audacity Garcia had made up his mind to destroy one of the lives standing between him and the treasure, in that public place, under the eyes of a hundred people. It had been no difficult matter to find out where de Vince was in the habit of dining, and Garcia had laid his plans accordingly. He had so contrived it that he could sit opposite his victim and shoot him coldly and deliberately with some form of pneumatic pistol. That such weapons were to be obtained, weapons almost as deadly as a revolver, Wendover knew perfectly well. The rest was a mere matter of nerve and courage, and the clerical attire had placed Garcia beyond the range of suspicion. No doubt he had concealed his weapon in the folds of his table napkin, and had shot down his victim through the barrier of the linen, as his hand apparently lay idly on the table. And in so doing the pellet from the pistol had severed one of the flowers in the vase of chrysanthemums on its flight. It was this broken flower that had given Wendover his clue, and he felt as sure of his ground now as if he had actually been a confederate in Garcia's confidence.

Now what was the next thing to be done? It would be futile to consult the Police, especially as Wendover had nothing but suspicion to go upon, and doubtless by this time Garcia's disguise had been safely hidden. Besides, to lay the matter before the authorities would be to disclose the whole history of the Brotherhood, and perhaps deprive Zena of the fortune to which she was undoubtedly entitled, to say nothing of the fact that he would be merely putting Garcia on his guard.

There was nothing for it, therefore, but to wait a favorable opportunity and call upon de Vince as soon as he was in a condition to receive visitors. He might be inclined to talk, he might be disposed to welcome the aid of one who would help him to bring Garcia to the end which he richly deserved. And meanwhile, he could make inquiries at the Ambassadors' Hotel. And with this resolve uppermost in his mind, Wendover smoked a final cigarette and went to bed. He would lunch at the Ambassadors' Hotel on the morrow.

He could not, however, resist the temptation of going round in the morning and giving Zena a call. He felt just a little guilty and ashamed of his eagerness, contrasting himself with a schoolboy who is in love for the first time. But he wanted to see the expression in those beautiful eyes, and, perhaps unconsciously, he was possessed by a desire to see if Zena looked as beautiful in the morning as she had done on the night of the dance.

But he need not have had any hesitation on that score. She was frankly pleased to see him, and took him up to that little room of hers as if it had been the most natural thing in the world. The place was a litter of odds and ends of colored silks and all those things which are so dear to the feminine heart, and on a table in the corner stood a sewing machine.

Wendover elevated his eyebrows.

"What is the necessity for all this?" he asked. "I had hoped you had turned your back on this slave-driving work for ever. Don't forget that you are quite rich now, a young woman who possesses her own fortune, to say nothing of the 50 conscience money that our friend sent you. Do you know, there must be some good in that man, after all."

Zena smiled happily.

"I feel this morning," she said, "as if all the world was full of good people. And don't forget, Paul, that it behoves me to be careful; 550 will not last for ever, and I have the future to think of. Suppose you fail?"

"Oh, I am not going to fail," Paul declared. "I shall see this thing through, and I shall win. And that is why I am sorry to find you ruining those beautiful eyes of yours with all this fine work."

"I like it, Paul. I am fond of my work. And besides, it keeps me from thinking. It keeps me from brooding and worrying about you."

"Oh, then, you do worry about me?"

"Of course, I do. You are the only friend I have in the world, and when I think of all your goodness to me I feel as if I could not do enough for you. And now, perhaps you understand why I want to go on with my work. I should prefer to have a little place in the country, but I must be somewhere near you. I like to be in touch with you all the time, where I can know exactly what is going on, and feel that you are safe."

"Oh, I shall be safe enough," Paul laughed. "Don't worry that pretty little head of yours about that. Still, it is good to know that someone is interested in me."

X - THE WINDOW OVER THE STUDIO

It was just before 1 o'clock the following day that Wendover strolled into the Ambassadors' Hotel. He was fortunate enough to find the same waiter who had been so useful to him on the night of the dance. A gold coin, and in indication that this was a confidential matter, unlocked the waiter's lips, and he spoke freely.

"Oh, yes, sir," he said. "Mr. Detmar, 'e stay frequently in ze 'otel. 'E come an' go from ze Continent an' e' always haf ze same suite of rooms."

"Did he dine here last night?" Wendover asked.

"'E did not dine at all, sir," the waiter responded. "Las' night 'e not very well. 'E go to 'is room about 7 o'clock with ze bad headache and they take 'im up tea an' toast for dinner, an' 'e say 'e was not to be called zis morning before ten o'clock. Then 'e breakfast in 'is room."

Here was information indeed. For Wendover was positively certain of the identity of the sham clergyman whom he had seen in the Cafe Montagne the night before. But it was up to him to say nothing to arouse the waiter's suspicions.

"Indeed," he said. "Did you see the gentleman last night in his bed-room? Did anybody see him?"

"I think not, sir. Only his friend, Mr. Ogilvy, a reverend gentleman who is a great friend of his. When he come for ze night as a rule 'e 'ave a bed made up for 'imself in Mr. Detmar's dressing-room."

"Mr. who?" Wendover asked. He had almost forgotten for the moment that Garcia passed in the hotel as Detmar. "Oh, yes, how stupid of me. Of course. So this Mr. Ogilvy came here yesterday, did he, and spent the night on a bed made up in Mr. Detmar's sitting room. Is he here now?"

"No, sir. 'E dine out last night an' when 'e come back about 10 'e gave orders to be called zis morning at 6 as 'e 'ad to catch an early train. 'E wanted no breakfast an' I suppose 'e went. I did not see 'im go. At zat hour in ze morning zere will be no one about, except perhaps a chamber-maid, and so many of our customers leave quite early."

Wendover saw it all quite plainly now. He could only admire the cunning way in which at every turn Garcia was covering up his tracks. No doubt he had used the clerical disguise on more than one occasion. The whole thing was simple and ingenious to a degree. Garcia had only to announce that his friend Ogilvy was coming to stay with him, and then to retire to his bedroom with orders not to be disturbed, and the whole scheme was complete. Behind his locked door he could change into the clerical disguise and leave the hotel openly and freely whilst the management were under the impression that the man they knew as Mr. Detmar was safe in bed.

As Wendover drove back to Hampstead again he was profoundly impressed with the task that lay before him. At any rate, he would have plenty of time to think out some scheme, for nearly a fortnight elapsed before he was able to meet de Vince, who evinced the greatest disinclination to see any strangers. He was much better, his landlady informed Wendover, but horribly shaky and nervous, and in constant dread of another attack on his life. It was only when Wendover placed his card in an envelope together with his half of the gold disc of the Brotherhood, and sent it in for de Vince's benefit, that the latter consented to see him, and even then only in the presence of his landlady. It was quite a week later before de Vince was persuaded that Wendover's intentions were friendly, and so far forgot himself as to see him alone.

"You have something important to say to me, I think," he said. "Something to do with the Brotherhood."

"On the contrary, something entirely to do with you," Wendover said coolly. "If you will allow me to sit down and talk to you quietly I will put all my cards on the table."

"Proceed, Mr. Wendover," de Vince said warily.

"Thank you. Now to begin with, I am not one of the Brotherhood. I know all about it, but I obtained my disc and the mask I was wearing on the night of the meeting by stratagem. They both belonged to the murdered man who was found in the Ambassadors' Hotel. How I got them matters nothing. The police profess not to know who that unfortunate man was. But I think you can guess."

De Vince showed signs of agitation.

"I'd rather hear from your lips," he said.

"Well, the man who was murdered was Leo Detmar. And the man who murdered him beyond the shadow of a doubt was John Garcia. And Garcia had the audacity to pass himself off at the meeting as the man he had killed, which he did, despite the fact that Leo Detmar allowed himself to be arrested so that Garcia could escape to England. Now I am the man who betrayed Garcia to the Swiss police. I did so because the man is an abandoned scoundrel, who more than once has betrayed those who employed him. He was arrested on a trivial charge, but I had hopes in the meantime of getting evidence that would hang the fellow. In time I should have done so. It was to follow him up when I knew he had escaped, that I took advantage of a piece of good fortune which enabled me to be present at that meeting of the Brotherhood. Whether Garcia knows that I am the man who betrayed him for the present matters nothing. What does matter is that Garcia has made up his mind to become the master of the fortune in the fireproof safe, and that he is planning to murder all the members of the Brotherhood so as to lead the way. With any luck next year he hopes to be present when the time lock runs out, and he hopes to be present in that room alone."

"You are a wonderful man, Mr. Wendover," de Vince cried.

"We need not discuss that for the moment. I see you quite agree with me, and that you now understand why I am here. In all probability my life is just as much at stake as yours. And that is why I am ready to assist you. And now, in proof of my bona-fides, I am going to tell you exactly what happened in the Cafe Montagne and just how that attempt was made on your life. Now, listen!"

Between the whiffs of his cigarette, Paul told his story. De Vince listened with mingled admiration and astonishment.

"You have got it," he cried, "by heaven, you have got it! I see you know the sort of man you had to deal with. I see you realize the deadly peril in which the three of us stand. Can you wonder that my nerves are all broken up, and that I creep about, afraid of my own shadow? I only dare to travel in a cab, and at night I lie awake, sweating and trembling. For this is the fourth time that the fiend has tried the same thing. And yet a year ago I did not know the meaning of the word fear. And you can help me-oh, yes. There is a place of safety for me here. It is a studio next door where there are thick bars to the windows and overhead a bedroom, the door of which is lined with steel like a safe. It was the whim of an artist who was mad, who had delusions that the anarchists of Russia were after him. There are bars to the bedroom window, too. It was in Paris that I heard this studio was to let, and I should have been established in it now but for that cursed scoundrel Garcia. I have a faithful man-servant who will do anything for me, and who would look after the house. In yonder desk you will find money. Take 100 and go over to the agent and arrange that I become the tenant at once. For that sum I can take over the lease and the furniture. Perhaps I shall be safe there-at any rate, I shall have a chance to recover my lost nerves."

Within an hour their transaction was completed, and de Vince was installed in his new home.

So far, so good. For the present, at any rate, it looked as if de Vince was absolutely safe from the cold blooded and implacable enemy whose aim and end in life was to run him down and utterly destroy him. There were others in the way of Garcia's ambition, of course, but probably he was devoting all his attention for the moment to his present victim, and the mere fact that his first attempt upon de Vince had ended more or less in failure would render him extra careful in the future.

There was always the temptation in Wendover's way to find out Garcia's disguise and watch him night and day until he had effected his purpose, so far as de Vince was concerned, and then, when the proofs were overwhelming, hand him over to the punishment that inevitably awaited him. This would mean that Garcia would be hanged, and Wendover's task reduced to one of the easiest proportions.

But he put his temptation away from him, nothing should induce him to win through at the cost of another man's life, however unworthy that life might be, and, for the next day or two, Wendover set himself down doggedly to watch carefully for the inevitable development on the part of the foe. It was part of his policy to keep out of de Vince's way for the present, until at any rate, the man could take a pull at his nerves and get himself in hand again.

The best part of a week passed before there was any sign of movement on Garcia's part; then, late one night, when Wendover was prowling about in the neighbourhood of the studio, he saw something that aroused his suspicions.

It seemed to him that, in the darkness, he could make out the outline of a dim figure creeping along, in the direction of the house, and, instantly, he followed it at a discreet distance. There was a possibility, of course, that the figure in front was Garcia's, and that he had come there bent on some murderous mischief. Still, it was no part of Wendover's programme at that moment to make himself known, so he stood on the grass and watched the figure in the neighbourhood of the front door till it seemed to him that he might disclose himself, then he advanced towards the house, carelessly humming a tune. The mysterious figure immediately vanished, and it was some minutes before Wendover deemed it prudent to strike a light.

Between the lock and the door-post were the plain marks of a chisel. Wendover whistled to himself softly.

"Garcia is losing no time," he murmured. "Evidently the game has begun afresh. Well, we shall see."

XI - THE LEADED PANE

It was a matter of weeks before Wendover succeeded in gaining the confidence of de Vince. There was something about the man that was both attractive and repulsive at the same time. He appeared to be generous and impulsive, but vain and selfish to a degree. He did not say much about the Brotherhood to which, Wendover gathered, he had at one time been loyal and enthusiastic. But those days apparently had long gone by, and now de Vince appeared to regard the Society more as a means of living than anything else. Apparently at one time the Brotherhood had consisted of over twenty, but in one way or another they had dropped away until only three or four remained. And, so far as Wendover could ascertain, only those he had met that fateful night at the Ambassadors' Hotel knew the secret of the time lock and the story of the treasure in the safe. It was nearly two months before Wendover was satisfied that this was the case.

Meanwhile de Vince had passed most of his time in his new house at Hampstead, painting fitfully and taking occasional journeys to town in the company of his man, without whom he never even went across the Heath. And in this time more than one attempt had been made upon his life. More than once Wendover had seen the man who called himself James Ogilvy hanging about in the neighbourhood. It was more than significant that the appearance of the man in clerical attire tallied with some attempted outrage in which de Vince was concerned. Then these futile attempts ceased and Wendover came to the conclusion that some deeper plot was on foot. Over three months had elapsed before the next sign came of Garcia's activity.

Outwardly at any rate, de Vince should have been safe enough. He was never seen alone, the small house at Hampstead was protected by the last thing in the way of bolts and bars and the studio in which de Vince spent most of his time was protected from the outside like a goal. De Vince's bedroom had windows of the old-fashioned type, small windows in leaded panes outside of which were steel bars, the door was lined with fireproof bronze, and burglar proof thermite steel, and fastened with a patent lock. The fireplace was so small that nothing larger than a cat could have come down the chimney.

It was only here at nights that de Vince felt really safe. Once he had locked himself in his bedroom he felt that he could defy the world. In moments when his nerves were at their worst he would lock himself in his stronghold and stay there for days together. He never ceased to whine and complain, never ceased to wonder what would become of him when once his resources were exhausted. Wendover did not ask what these resources were, but he could guess. De Vince was living on the thousand pounds which he had obtained at the last meeting of the Brotherhood. Occasionally when de Vince was at his worst he would implore Wendover to come round and dine with him and spend the night under his roof.

"I can't help it," he whined. "There was a time when I was as courageous as you are. And when I think of that fiend, and the way he is trying to track me down, my heart turns to water. And he will get me yet, he will have me in spite of all my precautions. Even if I call in the police it will come to the same thing. Don't laugh at me, Wendover. Stay the night like a good fellow, and be a friend. If anything happens to me, you have a spare key to my bedroom, and if you find me dead in bed some time, as you will, all my money and private papers are in the little black box on the mantelpiece. My disc is there, too. Curse the Brotherhood! Would to heaven I had never seen or heard of it."

Scenes like this occurred once or at twice a week, but November dragged through and Christmas was at hand, and, as yet Garcia had made no sign. Evidently he knew how to bide his time.

It was one night early in January, and de Vince was at his worst. His frayed nerves were all on edge, he was white and trembling, and his eyes were full of terror.

"You will come back and sleep here to-night," he implored. "You won't leave me alone, Wendover?"

"It shall be as you like," Wendover replied. "But I'm dining out this evening and going to the theatre afterwards with Miss Corroda, and very likely we shall sup at a restaurant at the finish. I can get back here by half-past twelve, if you will ask your man to sit up for me."

"Give Miss Corroda my kind regards," de Vince said. "Say that I have always done my best for her. If anything happens to me you will find over six hundred pounds in the little black box which I want you to give to her. Strictly speaking, it is her own money."

Wendover gave the desired promise and went his way. During all this time he had seen Zena once or twice a week, and though he had not breathed to her a single word with regard to his feelings, there was a subtle understanding between them, and it needed no speech on Wendover's part to show the girl how deeply she had touched his affections. And she was happy enough in a way. There was something infinitely uplifting and comforting in the knowledge that this man cared for her, and that she had someone in the future to protect and shield her on her way through the world. And yet with it all there was always the haunting dread that something might happen to Wendover, and that at any moment he might fall a victim to the merciless scoundrel who was slowly clearing the path to the treasure of the safe. It was in vain that Wendover made light of these fears, fears which, in his less sanguine moments, he shared himself.

But even if Garcia had penetrated his identity he knew perfectly well that there would be no attempt upon his life until both de Vince and Nikolo Petroff were cleared out of the way. Then it would be time for him to look to himself. And in the meantime through his agents he was gradually collecting together the evidence through which he hoped, if not to hang Garcia, at any rate to lay him by the heels for the rest of his natural life. And moreover, another set of agents were keeping Garcia under close observation. In his frequent visits to the Continent he was followed every step of the way, but latterly he was spending most of his time at the Ambassadors' Hotel, where he entertained largely and posed as a man who has made a large fortune and was now in a position to enjoy it. But even at this time he had his bad days, when he spent most of his time in his bedroom, and on such occasions the Rev. James Ogilvy was always more or less in evidence.

"We won't worry about him to-night at any rate," Wendover smiled. "We are quite safe for the present, and so far de Vince has met with no harm. And there is always a chance at any moment of my being in a position to get Garcia arrested by the Swiss or Italian police. So let us go and dine quietly at the Ritz, and go to the theatre afterwards. Courage, little girl, courage. You will be a rich heiress yet, and then I shall be afraid to come near you."

Zena laughed happily. Her cheeks were flushed with pleasure, her dark eyes gleamed like stars.

"In that case I would rather be as I am," she said. "What would the money be to me without you, Paul?"

"Are you making love to me?" Wendover asked.

"There's no occasion," the girl said simply. "I think that you and I understand one another from the first. I am not deceiving myself. And if ever you leave me! But, my dear boy, you will never do that."

"How well you know your power," Wendover whispered.

"Do I?" Zena laughed happily. "Well, perhaps I do. I think that every girl does, when once she realises herself. And yet there was a time when I was not aware that there was such a person as you in existence."

"Nor I you," Wendover said. "I was just casting about for something to do, some mere excitement to fill in the time, and I find by sheer chance, the great adventure of my life. If I had not been impudent enough to follow you that afternoon in Fleet Street—"

"If you had not, well, really, I don't want to think about it, Paul. I should be just struggling on in that little room of mine, fighting hard for a living, and with nothing but the dreariest fortune before me. And now, as you say, I am more or less of a capitalist—"

"Ah, that's just what I was going to talk to you about," Wendover said. "You have more than five hundred pounds, and I suppose a girl who has been brought up like you could live on about two pounds a week, and be quite well dressed into the bargain. You could make your own clothes—"

"I do," Zena smiled. "I made the dress I am wearing at the present moment. And I hope you think I look nice."

"You look lovely, as you always do," Wendover cried. "But surely a dress like that is sheer extravagance?"

"It would be if I bought it in a shop," the girl laughed. "It would cost pounds and pounds. As a matter of fact, it was all done for thirty shillings."

"Upon my word, Zena, you are wonderful. You might be a duchess, or, at any rate, a girl in a family where they have nothing to do except think about their clothes. Do you know, that you will make quite a sensation when we go into supper, and already some of my friends are asking me the name of that distinguished looking foreign princess that I have been seen with so frequently of late. Oh, it's a fact, I assure you; you've no idea how they envy me."

It was all utter nonsense, of course, but infinitely sweet to Zena, lying back by the side of the man she loved, the girl who, not very long ago, had shrunk back from the future, the future which she was almost afraid to face. And now, everything had changed, now she was armed against the world, in comfortable circumstances, and, but for the uncertainty and dread of what might happen to Wendover, there was not a cloud on the horizon. She sighed happily.

"Ah, Paul," she said. "You are very good to me. I don't know what I have done to deserve all the kindness I have received at your hands."

XII - A VAIN ENDEAVOUR

Zena looked back upon that evening afterwards as the happiest of her life. She was frankly and innocently conscious of her own beauty, and joyous in the knowledge that, in her simple evening dress and Neapolitan violets, she contrasted favorably with any woman there. And she was glad not so much for her own sake, but for Wendover's. She liked to see the love and pride of possession in his eyes, she was proud of his admiration, and content with the world as she found it. For the moment, at any rate, she had put all fear out of her mind, and gave herself over wholly to the enjoyment of the evening. There was a theatre afterwards, followed by a cosy little supper, and then the drive home in a taxi that was all too short.

Zena lay back in the corner of the cab, dwelling on the events of the evening. Wendover was talking to her, but she was hardly conscious of what he said. Then presently she knew that her hand was in his, and that his arm was about her waist. He bent to kiss her, and she gave her lips back to him as if it were the most natural thing in the world.

"Am I too bold?" Wendover asked.

"Oh, no. You know, you have known all the time that there never could have been anybody else. Between us there is no need for words. Don't spoil it by saying anything, Paul, because I can read your heart as easily as you can read mine. And I am so glad, so proud to give myself to you like this."

The rest of the drive was pure enchantment to Zena, and she parted presently from her lover without another word being said on either side. It was like some beautiful dumb play, like a famous comedy that Zena had once seen in a famous Paris theatre. Mere words would have spoilt it. They would come all in good time, but for the moment a love idyll like that did not call for them. It is not often that a girl finds the ideal lover, but it seemed to Zena at that moment that she had been picked out and exalted above other women.

Meanwhile Wendover drove back to Hampstead with his head in the clouds. He only came back to earth again as he stopped before the door of the studio and rang the bell. After a moment's hesitation, an inquiry as to who was there, de Vince's servant opened the door. His master had gone to bed, he said, though he had not yet put out the light.

"How is he to-night, Martin?" Wendover asked.

"Very nervous, sir. Very shaky and ill-tempered. He began to think that you were not coming. He had his supper in his bedroom, and I have just cleared the things away. Can I get anything for you, sir?"

"Nothing to eat," Wendover said. "You might leave out the tantalus, and a syphon of soda water, and then you can go to bed. I shan't want anything else."

De Vince's voice called out from the top of the staircase.

"Is that you, Wendover?" he asked. "Oh, all right, I only wanted to be sure that you had come back. I'm not coming downstairs. I've just had a sleeping draught, and I think I shall get a good night's rest."

He closed the bedroom door behind him, and Wendover heard the click of the patent lock. He sat there for an hour or more, smoking cigarettes to the accompaniment of a weak whisky and soda, sat there for an hour or so with his head in the air dreaming over the events of the evening. As he turned sleepily between the sheets of his bed he heard a distant clock striking the hour of two. Then he slept peacefully, for he knew not how long till it seemed to him that he was aroused by the sound of a heavy fall in the next room and a muffled scream. Just for a moment it occurred to him it that he was merely dreaming. Nothing could possibly be happening in the next room, no evil hand could reach out for de Vince there, and Wendover turned on the other side and prepared to sleep again. But he could not altogether rid himself of the uneasy feeling in his mind. He knew all about the steel-lined room and the heavy bars before the old-fashioned latticed windows. But he knew also of the man he had to deal with. He had a wholesome respect for Garcia's dogged tenacity and his infinite resource. Still he closed his eyes again and tried to sleep. But sleep refused to come to him, so at the end of a quarter of an hour he switched on his light and crept on to the landing. Then very gently he knocked on de Vince's door. He knocked again and again, but no reply came. No doubt de Vince was sleeping peacefully, no doubt the morphia tabloid had done its work. But Wendover was not satisfied.

He crept back to his room and took the duplicate key of de Vince's door from his pocket. He entered and switched on the light. In the full ray of the electric he could see de Vince propped up on his pillows with his face turned towards the window. There was a queer sort of convulsive grin on his face, his lips were drawn back, showing his teeth, in a snarl like that of a frightened dog who is driven into a corner and terrorised to the verge of danger. But no motion was there of the unfortunate man's chest, he had for some time ceased to breathe, though his limbs were still relaxed and the body was yet warm. There was no sign yet of rigor mortis. In the centre of de Vince's forehead was a tiny blue mark, not greater in circumference than a pea, but at the base of the skull there was a jagged hole, from which the deep indigo blood was still flowing freely. Beyond doubt de Vince had been shot dead as he lay asleep, or perhaps just at the moment as he had opened his eyes to the consciousness that all his precautions had been in vain. Anyway, the man was dead, and the one man in the world who knew how the thing had been done was gazing down at the corpse.

And yet Wendover did not know how it had been done. He was aware of the identity of the hand from which this foul blow had been struck, but as to the rest he was utterly and entirely puzzled. He stepped forward to lay his hand upon the bell, and then he paused. He would have to move slowly. There were other things to think of besides the manner in which de Vince had come to this end. There was Zena, for instance. And the story of the Brotherhood which must not be told yet. The household must be alarmed and the police called in presently, but there were certain things to be done first.

Wendover crossed the room and took from the mantelpiece the little black box. He knew that this contained de Vince's money and the disc of the Brotherhood. And these in no case could concern the police. He hid the black box in a place of safety and returned to the scene of the murder. He knew perfectly well that de Vince's door had been secure, for he had tried it before he himself had gone to bed. There were only two keys in the world to fit that door, a fact that had been guaranteed by the makers of the lock. The blind was down in front of the window, and behind it every pane of glass in the leaded frame was absolutely sound and intact. So, too, were the bars of the window. How, therefore, had this dastardly crime been accomplished? Here was the door safe and sound, the window undisturbed, and the blinds still down. And as for the chimney, no human being could possibly squeeze through here. And yet de Vince had been murdered, had been shot clean through the brain by a sure hand with a revolver. There could be no suggestion of suicide either, for the closest search of the bedroom disclosed no sign of a weapon. Nor was the key of his own door missing, for Wendover found it in the murdered man's trouser pocket. Throughout the house every door and window was securely fastened. The whole thing was so weirdly mysterious that Wendover shivered and a strange sensation crept up his spine. Then he called up the police on the telephone.

Indeed, it was absolutely necessary to call on the police now. The crime at the Ambassadors' Hotel could look after itself; the thing had been done beyond all recall, before Paul had come upon the scene, and before he had the least idea that he was about to embark upon the great adventure of love and danger that had changed the whole course of his life. But it seemed to him that it would be an imprudent thing to disappear now and detach himself from the strange circumstances that surrounded the death of de Vince. Besides, by so doing, he might place it beyond his power to avail himself of certain clues which had come into his possession.

Yes, he would call up the police and tell them just as much as it seemed to him that they were entitled to know. He would say nothing whatever about the safe and its contents, nothing whatever about Zena's father, and the strange circumstances which led to the depositing of all that treasure in the safe.

He could pose as a man who had met de Vince casually, and who had learnt something of the source of his terror. He could tell Scotland Yard authorities that de Vince was a man who had mixed himself up in some Socialist conspiracy, and that he was hiding from the vengeance of his colleagues. So far it would be quite safe to go, and this he could do without implicating himself in any way. He did not suppose, for a moment, that the Scotland Yard people would know anything about Garcia or the ramifications of the Brotherhood, and, so far, he knew that the Criminal Investigation Department had not connected the body of men who gathered in room No. 75 at the Ambassador's Hotel with the death of Leo Detmar.

It seemed almost incredible that the authorities had not blundered on their trail, or that the management of the Ambassadors' Hotel had not mentioned it, but there it was, and a few discreet inquiries made at Scotland Yard had served to confirm this impression in Wendover's mind.

He merely called up the police on the telephone, with the information that a mysterious occurrence had taken place at Hampstead, and that their presence was required immediately, then he sat down to wait, going over in his mind and arranging the details that he was going to disclose. It was nearly an hour later before he was told that someone wanted to see him. He saw a short, thick-set man, with a pair of observant eyes, and a quick, alert manner, who touched his cap.

"From Scotland Yard, sir," he said. "I think you are the gentleman that sent for me."

XIII - DE QUINCEY'S DIARY

It was in vain, of course, that the police sought for some tangible clue to London's latest sensational crime. Wendover might have had a good deal to say, but, for the moment, he was hanging back. Nothing was to be gained by discussing the affairs of the Brotherhood, and there was just a possibility of the murderer being brought to justice without giving Scotland Yard the whole of the facts. It might be necessary to do so later on, but for the moment Wendover was playing his own hand. To the inspector in charge of the case he simply posed as a recent acquaintance of the dead man, but he mentioned Garcia under the name of Detmar, and was frank enough with regard to the comings and goings of the Rev. James Ogilvy. About the Brotherhood and the secret of the safe he said nothing. It seemed to him that for the present he had given the authorities enough ground for arresting Garcia, but further than this he decided not to go.

But a visit to the Ambassadors' Hotel disclosed the fact that the man who called himself Detmar had disappeared, and that nothing was known of the Rev. James Ogilvy, except the fact that he had occasionally been the guest of the sham Austrian millionaire. And it is perhaps needless to say that Crockford's Clergy List contained no such name as James Ogilvy. For the present, at any rate, the police investigations had merely led into a blind alley.

But the inspector in charge of the case made certain discoveries which went far to satisfy Wendover as to the way in which the crime had been committed.

"I think I can tell you all about that, sir," the inspector said. "If you will come with me as far as the studio I fancy I can prove my theory."

"I shall be only too pleased," Wendover said.

The studio itself with the bedroom over had been built out at an angle to the house and the upper room, de Vince's bedroom, in fact, had a flat roof, coated with lead.

"Look here, sir," the inspector said. "If you will look at that drainpipe against the wall you will see that it has been recently climbed with the aid of irons. You can see where the paint has been scratched off, and the bricks scarred. In the darkness of the night the task would be an easy one to an able-bodied man, especially if he had studied his ground. And the rest was easy. The bedroom window is pretty close to the leads, and it would have been no difficult matter to attach a portable seat with ropes to the gutter so that the criminal could sit there comfortably in front of the window. Then with the aid of a painter's knife he could have turned back the lead from the latticed panes and removed half a dozen of them in a few minutes. There was no fear of being disturbed because the studio looks out over the open heath. Once this was done the blind could have been pulled aside through the bars, and a brilliant electric torch turned on the face of the man who was sleeping on the bed there. This torch would have been held in the left hand, and would have given a perfect view of the interior of the room. In his right hand the murderer had an automatic pistol to which a silencer was attached. Can't you see how easy it all was?"

"It does sound simple now," Wendover admitted.

"Simple as kiss your hand. With one shot the mischief was done. Then all the murderer had to do was to replace the blind and put those panes of glass back again and flatten the leads holding them with his knife. I know he did this because there are traces that the panes have been recently removed. Then the murderer goes about his business under the natural impression that he has left no trace behind. But though this is well enough in its way, it does not bring us any nearer to the arrest of the assassin, and I am very much afraid that it never will."

It looked as if the inspector's prophecy was likely to be verified, for the end of March came and no trace of a Detmar, or rather Garcia, had been found, and thus nine months had elapsed since the meeting of the Brotherhood at the Ambassadors' Hotel. With all his caution, Wendover found himself at fault. By this time Zena had moved into more comfortable quarters which the possession of her money had enabled her to take. But she was still restless and anxious, and fearful lest at any moment the long arm of Garcia would reach out of the darkness and deal her lover some mortal injury.

But there was another man to be got rid of first in the person of Nikolo Petroff, though possibly he had already been dealt with. And Wendover could have given a good deal to have been sure of the fact. Sooner or later he would have to know, and one day the knowledge came to him from a source which was altogether unexpected.

It came in the form of a letter from Newquay addressed to de Vince at the Hampstead studio. As it was put in the letter-box of the studio of which Wendover still possessed the key, he opened it without hesitation. It was not for him to know that it came from the very man for whom he was seeking. And it left absolutely nothing untold.

Evidently de Vince had been corresponding with Petroff, and the dead man's last letter had been forwarded to him to an address at Drayton in Virginia. In reply Petroff apologized for the fact that the letter had been delayed in transmission. Petroff, it appeared, was at present hiding from some threatening danger in an ideal little village near Newquay, and from the contents of the letter Wendover decided the fact that Petroff stood in the same deadly fear of Garcia as de Vince himself had done.

"I may tell you, my dear friend," the letter ran, "that I have no intention at present of leaving these safe quarters. It was an accursed day for us when that money was placed away in the fireproof safe, and that black scoundrel made up his mind to rid the world of us so that the treasure might be his. But I have escaped him now, and he and London will never see me again. And I have found something to do, my friend. I have made the acquaintance of a charming old professor of literature, an American, who has obtained a number of unpublished manuscripts, written by the famous author, Thomas de Quincey. I always had literary tastes, as you know, and arranging these letters for the press for my friend, the Professor, affords me not only a congenial occupation, but a living as well. You were an admirer of de Quincey, I think. It will be news to you that he once attempted to commit suicide by poisoning himself. I have seen the original letter; in fact, I have just made a copy of it for the professor from the original manuscript. It was found by de Quincey's side on one occasion when he had taken an overdose of laudanum. But all this may not interest you.

"But why not come down here and join me? It is a charming and ideal spot, and the old professor is delightful company. I can give you a room in my cottage."

There was much more to the same effect, but Wendover was satisfied. The more he turned this matter over in his mind the more sure he was that behind all this was some deep-laid plot for the taking off to Petroff. Then, like a flash of lightning it burst on Wendover's understanding that here was Garcia's work again, and that the old professor was none other than that clever scoundrel in a fresh disguise. Here was some scheme in which laudanum or opium was being used with deadly effect; perhaps the mischief was already done.

An hour later Wendover was on his way to Paddington to catch the next train to the Cornish Riviera.

Of course, it was no more than a mere surmise on Wendover's part, one of those deductions that come like a flash of inspiration every now and again, to those engaged in criminal investigations, and which mark the difference between the ordinary policeman and the born detective. Wendover had nothing to go upon, except by his own great good fortune he had come upon a letter which showed quite plainly that Petroff had not only been in constant communication with de Vince, but that he, too, had in some strange way blundered upon a clue which had given him a clear indication of Garcia's murderous designs.

And perhaps Petroff, too, had known something of this scheme that Garcia had put up with a view to blinding his colleagues, and getting the unfortunate Detmar to impersonate him in a Swiss gaol. Clearly the scoundrel had not been so cunning as he thought, and, clearly, several of the Brotherhood at any rate had obtained some inkling of what was going on. Therefore, there was nothing for it now, but to get down to Cornwall without delay. But, first of all, before he left London, it would be only an act of prudence to call on Zena and tell her what he was about to do. She listened to him quietly enough, her eyes were brave and steadfast, but, at the same time she turned pale and faltered as she spoke.

"Oh, do be careful, Paul," she said. "I dread the idea of your placing yourself in that man's power. And I am quite sure that he knows all about you. I am quite sure he knows who Paul Wendover is, and that he is just as eager to get rid of you as anybody else. He has made up his mind that your turn is to come as soon as he has got rid of the others, and, by going down to Cornwall to that lonely village you are placing yourself entirely in his power. He might lure you to the edge of a cliff and murder you."

"I don't think so," Paul said confidently. "To begin with, if my suspicions are correct, I shall have the advantage of knowing what I have got to deal with. And again, if Garcia is really posing as this harmless old professor of literature, he will never dream for a moment that I have penetrated his disguise. I can assure you, my dearest girl, I have been in greater danger than this. Don't look so unhappy, Zena, don't make me feel sorry that I told you. Come, be the brave little girl you were on the night of Detmar's death, and wish me good luck in my task. And if you—"

"Oh, I know, I know," the girl cried. "You want me to give you a kiss. Well, a hundred, if you like. And write to me every day. I shall know no peace till you return."

XIV - A FORGED LETTER

It was nine or ten days later, and Wendover found himself comfortably settled down in an old farm-house on the outskirts of the quiet village where Petroff had taken up his quarters. In a place so small it would be no difficult matter to make the acquaintance of Petroff and inform him that he, Wendover, had been with de Vince on the night of his death.

It was clear enough that Petroff was shocked and frightened at this information. In the circumstances he promised readily enough not to mention this matter to a soul, not even to Professor Galloway, the charming old gentleman in whose employ Petroff was at that moment.

"I am not astonished that you are disturbed," Wendover said, "and I am sure you have guessed who was the author of your unhappy friend's death."

"It was Garcia," Petroff said hoarsely.

"Of course. And it was Garcia who murdered Leo Detmar at the same time that he was pretending to be Detmar himself. I had all the information from de Vince, and I am as sure as you are that Garcia is looking for you all over the world to serve you the same way. Of course, it is the money in the safe that he is after, and to obtain possession of that he is ready to wade up to his neck in crime. But for the moment, at any rate, you appear to be safe so long as you tell your secret to no one. Now I want you to introduce me to this old professor as a friend of yours and just leave it at that. I am curious to see that man."

An evening or two later the meeting took place. Outwardly, at any rate, Petroff had not exaggerated the charming manner and quaint personality of the man who called himself Professor Galloway, late English lecturer of an American University. He was an old man with abundant white hair and beard, an old, benevolent-looking man, who appeared to survey life pleasantly through a pair of large gold-rimmed spectacles. His English was perfect, with just the trace of a foreign accent, which he attributed to his mother, who had been Spanish-American. And just at that moment he appeared to be entirely wrapped up in his recent discovery of the de Quincey documents, which he declared that he had picked up in an old book-shop in the older quarters of New York.

"They will be a revelation to the public," he said, as they sat at supper in Petroff's tiny cottage. "And my friend, Petroff, is going to share the glory of this great find. In fact, he has been invaluable to me. You see, I am old and shaky, and my handwriting is not what it was. And therefore, Petroff has made separate copies of all those letters for the publishers. Some day, perhaps to-morrow, I will show you the original letters that de Quincey wrote after he had taken that overdose of laudanum. A disjointed fragment, but in the great man's own handwriting. But when I get on this hobby I can talk of nothing else. You are making a long stay here, Mr. Wendover, in this delightful spot?"

"It all depends," Wendover said evasively. "I should like to stay here a week or two, but I may have letters calling me away at any moment. But I shall be here till the end of the week-possibly longer."

Wendover spoke easily enough, but he was puzzled all the same. There were moments now and again when this man strongly reminded him of Garcia, but so far he could not be sure of his ground. If this man really were Garcia, then, indeed, he was a consummate actor, in addition to his other gifts, for so far he was keeping up his character to perfection. And so a week went by without anything happening to confirm Wendover's suspicions and without a single sign that Professor Galloway was anything but what he pretended to be.

Still, Wendover had no intention of allowing it to go at that. He carefully watched the man who called himself Professor Galloway, and, at the same time, assumed the air of a man who lives only in the moment, and has no concern for the morrow. More than once he found an opportunity of being alone with the professor; more than once they rambled together along the granite cliffs beyond the little fishing village, and talked together casually, as men will. Wendover spoke freely of his own work on the 'Daily Herald,' and of the various adventures he had gone through on behalf of that paper. He even mentioned certain anarchists he had met, and how he had laid himself out to lull their suspicions to sleep and worm himself into their confidence. For it was no part of his game to try and delude the astute and clever man whose identity was hidden behind a benevolent head of white hair and a pair of spectacles. And Garcia, if Garcia it was, listened and chuckled, and asked the most innocent questions, with the air of a boy on the beach discussing adventures with some old sailor.

"Ah, Mr. Wendover," the Professor said. "Do you know I find this most entertaining. You are opening up a new field to me, for I am almost ashamed to confess that I did not know there was so much wickedness in the world. You see, ever since I was a boy at school, I have cared for nothing but books, and I lived among old manuscripts till I am as dusty and old-fashioned as they are themselves."

As the Professor spoke, he chuckled and choked over his own poor little joke, and looked like a benevolent old gentleman who has never come in contact with crime or trouble throughout the whole of his easy and tranquil life. As a bit of acting, the whole thing was splendid, and Wendover was not grudging in his secret admiration.

"Yes, Professor," he said. "It is just as well that you should know these things. Some of these people may come your way, and then you will know how to deal with them."

The professor laughed like a boy.

"Indeed I shouldn't, Mr. Wendover," he said. "All this is very interesting, no doubt, but I am afraid, as a lesson that it would be thrown away. Now, what could I do with a revolver, for instance? It would be far more dangerous to me than to the man at the other end of it. And I am far too old for this sort of thing. I am very, very old."

He chuckled and wheezed, while Wendover watched him carefully. He felt that his time would come yet. For not one moment was he going to relax any vigilance.

Then there came an autumn night following a calm tranquil day on which Wendover had been out all the afternoon with a gun in his hand, and when he had finished his frugal supper he walked as far as Petroff's cottage with a view to a chat. Petroff had apparently just finished his supper, for the plates and dishes were piled up on a little side table, and at the writing desk, in the centre of the room, under a hanging lamp, was the tenant of the cottage with a mass of papers. The professor smiled as he looked up, but there was no welcome in his eye; indeed, he seemed rather annoyed at the interruption.

"I am intruding?" Wendover said.

"Well, perhaps, for once you are," the professor replied. "It is a rude thing to say, but you will pardon me. My publishers have telegraphed today for a portion of the manuscript, and I am very anxious to get it off by the mail in the morning. So perhaps, my dear sir—"

"I understand perfectly," Wendover said. "I will come round again in the morning."

With this he turned away and vanished into the night. Without quite knowing why, he felt restless and anxious. He had an idea that the trouble was approaching its crisis. But he could do nothing; in the circumstances it was impossible to interfere. He went to bed presently, his mind full of strange forebodings. Nor was he wrong!

Just after breakfast that following morning Professor Galloway came hurrying up to the farm house in a state of great distress and pitiable agitation.

"I am so pleased to have found you in, Mr. Wendover," he said, "for a most terrible thing has happened. My dear friend, Petroff, has committed suicide."

Wendover reeled back, sick and dizzy.

"Impossible," he cried. "He was the last man in the world to do anything of the sort. If he is dead, then you may be sure that he has been murdered."

"I wish I could think so. But the evidence of suicide is too strong. I left our poor friend last night at half-past ten, apparently in the best of health. When I looked into the cottage this morning I found him dead in his chair. Apparently he had not moved since I left him. By his side was a two-ounce bottle of laudanum, enough to kill half a dozen men. The bottle was nearly empty, and by the side of it a sheet of notepaper with a few lines in Petroff's handwriting to say that he could not keep fighting a mental trouble that is overpowering him any longer, and that he had decided to take his life. For his sake I would hush this matter up if I could, but you will see that such a course is out of the question. But would you not like to look into the matter for yourself?"

Petroff sat in his chair by the side of his table, quite dead. There was the empty bottle by his side, and the letter explaining the tragedy. And as Wendover bent to read it the blood was beating like drums in his head, for now he could see the whole thing plainly. Those de Quincey's letters were absolute forgeries, forgeries so cunningly contrived that, in copying one of them, Petroff had proclaimed in his own handwriting that he had destroyed himself, and there was the evidence to prove it in black and white. No doubt this miscreant had mixed enough laudanum with Petroff's supper to kill him, or perhaps he had been stunned with a blow, and the laudanum subsequently injected in his body.

It was some time before Wendover could pull himself together and look the actual murderer quietly in the face. He glanced up just in time to catch a murderous gleam in the other man's eyes, and then it vanished as quickly as a dream. And now Wendover knew beyond the shadow of a doubt that behind those glasses Garcia was gazing at him.

XV - THE REV. JAMES AGAIN

All that Wendover could do for the moment was to drop his eyes before those of the man opposite him, as if he himself had done something to be ashamed of, and could not meet the glance of the other. But, sooth to say, just at that moment, he was honestly, horribly afraid lest the sham professor should read in his eyes any suggestion that he had even a glimmering of the ghastly truth.

He wanted to be alone to think, to work this thing out and grasp the full meaning of Garcia's latest crime. In spite of the steady state of his nerves, and the fact that he had been forearmed against crimes of this kind, he was shaken and shocked, and perhaps for the first time a little doubtful of his ability to get the best of the terrible force that was arrayed against him. But he must not show this. He must not let Garcia imagine for a moment that that clever disguise of his had been penetrated. He turned his back upon the other and, walking across the floor of the room, stood for some moments gazing out to sea, with the air of a man who is battling with himself and fighting against the horror of it.

He might have turned and thrown himself upon the murderer who was grinning behind his back. He was far the more powerful man of the two, and had little to fear in an encounter with Garcia. He might have torn the disguise from the other's shoulders and accused him there and then of the terrible crimes which could be laid to his account. But then, if he did this, where were his proofs? He could only prove that Garcia was masquerading as an old professor, which could not have connected him in any way with the deaths of Petroff and de Vince, and besides, there, not many yards away, lay the evidence of suicide in Petroff's own handwriting. It had been a diabolically clever plot, and had succeeded, as such crimes generally do, when backed by matchless courage and audacity.

And again, such a course as an instant exposure must inevitably lead to the police being called in, and that was precisely what Paul didn't want. The greater part of his task was to recover for Zena the fortune to which she was morally entitled, and if the authorities took a hand in the game the money might be lost. There was nothing for the moment, then, but to play for a time, and to assume that Garcia was innocent of the whole business. When Wendover turned from the window again, there was nothing but regret in his eyes and a gravity befitting the tragic occasion.

"This must be a great shock to you," he said.

"Oh, indeed it is," Garcia responded glibly. "I had a great liking for that poor fellow, and from the very first we have got on well together. And I am an old man Mr. Wendover, and things like these disturb me terribly. There will be an inquest, of course, at which I suppose we shall both have to give evidence, not that there is any mystery about it at all. That poor fellow committed suicide, undoubtedly."

"Unfortunately, one can come to no other conclusion," Paul said. "He must have been out of his mind for a long time. How frequently these things happen, and no one guesses for a moment that the mind is unhinged. Perhaps you had better leave matters to me. I will see the police and the doctor, and take everything I can off your hands."

Garcia expressed himself to be exceedingly grateful. He seemed to be bowed and broken, and utterly unnerved by the tragic event. But ever and again there was just the suggestion of a triumph in his eyes, just the fleeting glance of the rascal who has got the best of the other man, and secretly rejoices in the fact. Evidently he was quite under the impression that Paul was utterly deceived.

The police came presently, followed by the local doctor, and on the next morning the usual inquiry took place. It was quite a formal affair, lasting not more than an hour or two, with none too many questions asked, for, naturally, there were no suspicions of foul play, and according to the Coroner, the duty of the jury was plain. At the end of an hour they brought in the usual verdict, and two days later the remains of the unfortunate Petroff were laid to rest in the village churchyard, followed by Wendover, who was the only mourner, the sham professor declaring that he was too utterly prostrated to attend. He did not know what he was going to do, he told Paul later on in the day. No doubt he would get over the shock in time, and meanwhile his work must stand still until he could find someone to take the place of his late secretary.

"I shall stay here till to-morrow," he explained, "indeed. I may remain here for the rest of the summer. I have had a letter from Plymouth in reply to a telegram of mine, from a friend who is recommending me a secretary. I think I will go to Plymouth and see this man. I could walk along the cliff and catch the carrier's cart to Wadebridge."

And that was the last time that Paul saw Garcia, at any rate in the guise of Professor Galloway. At the end of the second day he had not returned, and inquiries as to his whereabouts elicited the information that he had not caught the carrier's cart at all. He had been seen going along the cliffs in the direction of the village, and there all trace of him ceased. There was a certain place on the cliffs that pointed to the act that someone had slipped there, and, later in the day, some fishermen, scaling the cliffs, had picked up a cap and part of a watch chain which had been identified as the property of the sham professor, and later on a pipe and a pocket-book were washed up by the sea. It was quite evident, therefore, that another tragedy had taken place, and that the unfortunate professor had been the victim of a distressing accident.

That the body would be recovered the local coastguard was doubtful. It was rarely, indeed, that the remains of any drowned person ever came ashore there, and nobody questioned that the professor was dead.

Nobody, at any rate, with the exception of Wendover, who believed nothing of the kind. He was quite convinced that Garcia had disappeared in this mysterious manner so that he should not be tracked. And Paul was convinced of this by the finding of a white wig and a pair of spectacles which had been half buried in a pile of sand by the side of some gorse bushes. The whole thing had been arranged by the sham professor to cover up his tracks. The next day Paul was in London.

For the moment, at any rate, he was at a loose end. He knew he would have to wait till Garcia showed himself again, which he would be certain to do before long, seeing that there were two other men to be accounted for-the man with the orange-colored hair, and the individual with the throbbing lip. Till these were satisfactorily accounted for it would be utterly impossible for Garcia to complete his designs upon the safe.

On his way to town, Paul made up his mind what to do. Some instinct told him that Garcia would not be far away from the Ambassadors' Hotel, and there he booked a bedroom for a night or two, after which he went eagerly off in search of Zena.

She had gone out of town for a few weeks to a little cottage in the country, where she was holiday making and doing a little designing work at the same time. She welcomed Paul with every sign of delight.

"Oh, I am so glad to see you again," she said. "All the time you have been away from me, I have not known a moment's peace. I am ever thinking about that dreadful man, and the danger that you stand in. I am sure that he knows you, and that, when the others are out of the way, your turn will come. Paul, do oblige me, do give the whole thing up. I should be quite happy down here, if you would."

"Give it up! Never!" Paul cried. "Not even for you. Besides, it would be a cowardly thing, knowing what I do of Garcia. My dear child, you tempt me terribly. It would be delightful to retire somewhere down here, and live with you happily ever afterwards. But I have a plain duty before me. That man must be tracked down and utterly destroyed for the wild beast that he is. And, after this last affair, I am all the more determined."

Zena turned pale.

"Another tragedy?" she murmured. "Don't forget that I haven't heard from you for days."

"Yes, another one. Poor Petroff is no more. Sit down and I'll tell you all about it."

Zena listened with horror in those splendid eyes of hers to the grim story of Garcia's latest crime.

"Yes," she said presently. "I suppose you must go on. You would be a criminal too, if you left that man unpunished. My dearest boy, I am not thinking about the money at all. Now what are you going to do next?"

"Well, I am putting up, for the moment, at the Ambassadors' Hotel," Paul exclaimed. "You know, Garcia used to make his headquarters there. It is a great place where no questions are asked, and he would be comparatively safe there. I told you all about that cunning dodge of Garcia's phantom friend, who called himself the Rev. James Ogilvy. Now, I have a fancy that I shall see the Rev. James Ogilvy again."

It was late in the evening before Wendover found himself peacefully dining in the hotel. He had taken the precaution of obtaining a seat where he would be looked after by the same waiter who had given him information once or twice before. The big dining room was crowded with guests, and it was a long time before Paul noticed anything out of the common. Then presently, just before 9 o'clock, a little man in clerical garb came almost shyly in, and seated himself unobtrusively at table, just inside the door. He glanced about him in a mild sort of way, and it seemed to Paul that there was peculiar smile about the corners of his clean shaven mouth as he looked in his direction. It might be fancy on his part, but Paul was taking no chances.

"Waiter," he said. "I may be wrong, but I rather fancy I know that clerical gentleman by the door. Do you happen to know his name? Is he staying here?"

"Oh, yes," the waiter said. "He frequently stays here. He is a friend of the millionaire I told you about, Mr. Leo Detmar. He is the Rev. James Ogilvy."

XVI - THE MAN WITH THE THROBBING LIP

Paul deliberately turned his back upon the man in the clerical attire. He had found out all he wanted to discover for the moment. He had come on the track of Garcia again, and he felt that he could afford to wait for developments. That scoundrel had been over-cunning, and it would be no fault of Paul's if he gained anything by his last attempt to cover up his tracks. He was staying in the hotel, too, and occupying, no doubt, the bedroom that was usually in the possession of the man who passed for Leo Detmar; in other words, disguised as the Rev. James Ogilvy, he was sleeping in his own room-the room leading up to the same corridor in which was situated No. 75, where stood the famous safe. It was no difficult matter for Paul to make arrangements to have his own bedroom changed into the same corridor, and this he did without delay.

It seemed to him that all he had to do now was to keep a careful eye upon Garcia, who would feel perfectly safe in his present guise, and hang about till the next victim came along. And, doubtless, the next victim was not far away, or Garcia would not be seated there tranquilly dining. And that the next victim would be either the orange-haired man, or the man with the throbbing lip, Paul felt certain as he was that the sun would rise upon the morrow.

And he had not long to wait, either, for an hour or so later, whilst he was enjoying a cigar in the smoking room, and keeping his eyes open, there entered a young man in the guise of a Parsee. His face was dark, he wore a heavy moustache and beard, and upon his head was a white turban. And this foreigner had scarcely taken his seat in the smoking-room before the shrinking figure of the Rev. James Ogilvy came quietly in. From under his eyebrows Paul could see the malignant joy that beamed in Garcia's eyes as they fell upon the man in the white turban. It was only for an instant, however, then the gleam had vanished, and the sham clergyman lighted a cigarette and subsided behind a paper in a distant corner of the room. The man in the turban sat down close to Wendover, and presently the latter spoke to him.

Quite naturally, they glided into conversation. The stranger gave the name of Ramsi, and volunteered the information that he was a student at Cambridge University where he hoped to take a degree. Meanwhile he was enjoying a long vacation with certain friends in London, and in a day or two was proceeding to Brancaster in Norfolk, where he hoped to spend an enjoyable month on the golf links.

"You have played the game long?" Paul asked.

"About three years," the Indian explained. "I did not take it up till I was just forty, which is rather a pity, because that is a little late in life for so great a game. Still, I have managed to get down to scratch, and if I am at Cambridge next year, I hope to play for the University. Perhaps you are a golfer yourself, Mr. Wendover."

"Indeed I am," Paul said. "As a matter of fact, I have played for Cambridge. And I know the splendid links at Brancaster by heart. I envy you."

"Then why not come along," the Indian smiled.

"It is just possible that I may," Paul said drily. "That is, in a day or two. I am not certain of my movements yet. If I can manage it I will run down for the week-end and have the pleasure of a round with you."

"I should be delighted," the Indian said. "I have all my clubs with me, and am going there to-morrow."

Paul glanced over his shoulder; he could see that the man in the clerical attire was following the conversation with a close interest. Why, he wondered, why was Garcia so keen upon this foreigner, and what connection could he possibly have had with the Brotherhood? But presently a little incident happened that shed a more or less obscure light on the situation. Taking a matchbox from his waistcoat pocket, the Indian dropped something that tinkled on the floor, and, as Paul stooped to pick it up, he saw that it was no less than a segment of a gold coin, marked with a figure three; the sign of the Brotherhood, without a shadow of a doubt. Without comment, and without explanation, the stranger thanked him gravely, and restored the fragment to his pocket again.

Here, on the face of it, was another complication, here apparently was a fresh member of the Brotherhood of whom Paul knew nothing. There was no reason at all, so far as he could see, why the Brotherhood should not embrace every nationality, but it looked like complicating matters, and Paul was puzzled and a little worried accordingly.

But he showed no sign of what was passing in his mind, till the stranger rose and declared that it was time for bed. And when Paul casually asked him the number of his room, he was not surprised to discover that it was close to the one occupied by the Rev. James Ogilvy. As a matter of fact, it was back-to-back with his own, for the rooms were built in blocks, so that the doors on either wing faced into corridors, and high up in each bedroom, as Paul presently discovered, was a ground glass transam, evidently inserted for the purpose of ventilation, so that it was possible, by placing a chair on the dressing table, to get a glimpse into the next bedroom.

The Indian had disappeared at length, and presently the man, who called himself the Rev. James Ogilvy, vanished in his turn. He had hardly left the smoking-room before Wendover was after him. He saw the individual whom he now knew to be Garcia, creep along the corridor past his own bedroom and turn down the passage, at the end of which was room No. 75, Paul turned into one of the little fern-lined alcoves and watched.

At the end of half-an-hour Garcia returned, and closed the door of his bedroom behind him. Beyond doubt, he had been in the mysterious chamber for some purpose or another, perhaps to tamper with the lock of the safe. At any rate, he had been there on some illicit errand, and, before he slept, Paul decided to know what it was.

It was not a difficult matter, seeing that he himself possessed a latch-key to open the door, and as it was very late now, and no one was about, it would be possible to get into the room without arousing suspicion, or coming in contact with any belated servant. He crept very cautiously along the corridor till he came to the door. The place was as silent as the grave, and there was no sign of anyone near. Then, boldly, Wendover plunged his key in the latch, and entered the room. He fumbled for a moment or two until he found the switch, and flooded the room with light. He saw that the heavy curtains were closely drawn, and that it was not possible for anyone outside to know that the apartment was tenanted, and then, feeling perfectly secure, he proceeded to look about him.

The room was neat and clean. There was no sign that it had been occupied for months. The clock on the mantel-piece had run down, and, so far as Paul could judge, the safe had not been tampered with. There were no marks or signs of scratches on the lock, and no signs that anyone had been there for months, except a tiny trace of grey powder on the beautifully brushed carpet, a dust of cigarette ash, which had obviously been dropped there since the room was last in the hands of the cleaner. Paul smiled as his eyes fell on this, he smiled again as he saw the end of a cigarette lying in the fire place. This, obviously, had been recently pitched there by Garcia, in a careless moment, evidently feeling, no doubt, that there had been no reason for precaution.

"Ah, well," Paul murmured to himself. "These are the little mistakes that even the greatest criminals make sometimes. Not that it leads to anything, or tells me much, except that that scoundrel has been here. Now, I wonder what he was after. He was taking a risk in coming here, as I have done. However, the safe seems to be all right. I am sufficient of a detective to see that the lock has not been tampered with, and, apparently they have nothing to worry about here till the year is up, which is only a month or two now, by the way. I am frankly puzzled. I would give a good deal to know who this man is who calls himself Ramsi-and what connection he has with the Brotherhood. I have no doubt the name is assumed, indeed, in this extraordinary tangle I shouldn't be at all surprised to find that he is not a Parsee at all, and that the whole thing is a disguise. But I suppose his golf is all right, and I presume he is a student at Cambridge. Otherwise he would never have challenged me to go down to Brancaster and play with me. Well, I suppose I shall know in time."

With which Paul turned off the lights, and made his way, with all due caution, in the direction of his bedroom. He encountered no one by the way. So far he had made no slip, and once the door of the bedroom was closed behind him he turned on the lights and sat down on his bed to smoke a thoughtful cigarette and go over the events of the evening.

He was utterly puzzled. He abandoned his train of thought presently and proceeded to undress himself. As he turned off his own light, he could see the glimmer from the bedroom on the far side shining through the transam, and from this he knew that the Parsee was still up, or perhaps he was in the habit of burning his light all night. Paul lay on his back, idly wondering what the man in the bedroom beyond the transam was doing, whether he was asleep or not, or wondering whether he were worried in his turn..

Then, with a muttered cry, Paul rolled out of bed, and, as well as he could in the darkness, and as noiselessly as possible, proceeded to place a chair on his dressing-table and climb up on it, so that by pushing the transam a little on one side he could get a glimpse of the adjoining bedroom. With a little trouble he worked his head so far forward that he could see the bed with the man lying on it. Apparently he was fast asleep, for he was breathing regularly, and a gentle snore broke the silence. His turban was off, and so were the black beard and moustache, so that his face lay exposed to the light.

"Ah!" Paul exclaimed. "Ah!"

For the sleeper was the man with the throbbing lip.

XVII - THE INDIAN SPEAKS

Wendover came quietly down from his post of observation and crept back into bed. His discovery had not surprised him; indeed, he had expected something of the kind, though it had come quicker than he had anticipated, and it confirmed his worst suspicions. He had not expected, of course, to blunder straight away upon the identity of the man with the throbbing lip, but he had looked forward to little trouble in finding some member of the Brotherhood concealed behind that white turban and that luxuriant black beard.

Up to a certain point everything was clear enough. There was no doubt that Garcia, posing as the Rev. James Ogilvy was clear in his mind as to what he was doing, and, beyond question, he had penetrated the Indian's disguise. He knew, of course, that he was dealing with the man with the throbbing lip, and would not rest until he was out of the way. Once this was done there was only the man with the orange-colored hair to be dealt with, and Wendover did not doubt that he was not very far away. There might be others, of course, standing between Garcia and the precious contents of the safe, but Wendover had always had a feeling that he had come in contact with every surviving member of the Brotherhood on that eventful evening nine months ago, when they had all met in room No. 75. But that was a question for the future.

He lay back in the darkness there for an hour or two, working the matter out in his mind. He remembered now that the man with the throbbing lip had been dark and swarthy, and that the restless eyes behind his mask had been black and piercing. No doubt the man was conscious of his danger, no doubt since that fateful evening he had adopted eastern dress and moustache and beard for some pressing reason, and, no doubt, he knew that his life was in danger. And before Wendover slept he was quite clear as to what he was going to do.

He came down to breakfast in the morning fully alert, and glanced about him in search of the shrinking figure of the Rev. James Ogilvy. It came presently, with every sign of hurry about him, and sat down to a hasty breakfast. By his side was a timetable, which he studied carefully, and glanced hastily at his watch from time to time. Then he summoned a waiter to his side, and ordered a taxi. Wendover made a sign to his own favorite waiter.

"Look here," he said. "Do you want to earn half-a-crown? Because, if you do, it's yours."

The waiter grinned amiably.

"Anything you like, sir, of course," he said.

"Then keep your eye on the reverend gentleman over yonder. Unless I am greatly mistaken he is leaving the hotel this morning. Isn't that so?"

"Oh, yes, sir. I saw his bag and golf clubs come down."

Wendover whistled to himself. He was glad to hear the information as to the golf clubs, because it cleared the way and explained things wonderfully.

"Very well," he said. "You follow that gentleman to his taxi, and ascertain what station he is going from. It is very likely that his bag is already labelled, and if you can find out where it is labelled to, I'll give you an extra half-crown. Now then, off you go."

The man came back presently with a smile on his face, and his hand already outstretched.

"I have got it, sir," he said. "The gentleman has gone to Liverpool Street station on his way to a place called Brancaster. There was a label on his bag, and he is going to stay at the Grand Hotel."

Wendover handed over the two half-crowns with a distinct impression that they were not wasted. He could afford to linger over his breakfast now, and wait for the evening express, sure in the knowledge that he would see the Parsee before he left, and discuss matters with him, free from the prying eyes of the man in clerical attire. He had nearly finished, and had his cigarette case in his hand when the Indian entered. He smiled presently, as he saw Wendover.

"You won't change your mind?" he asked. "And come with me. I am going down by the 5 o'clock train."

"Do you know," Wendover drawled. "I rather think I will. I can put my business on one side for a day or two, and the weather is very tempting. Where are you staying?"

"There is only one place to stay in Brancaster," the Indian said. "That is the Grand Hotel. It's sure not to be full just yet, but perhaps you had better take the precaution of telephoning for a room. And then, if you will meet me at Liverpool Street Station at a quarter to five—"

"You can count upon me," Wendover said emphatically.

He went his way presently, and the rest of the morning was spent at the office of the 'Herald.' He was at Liverpool Street a little before the time fixed where, with the aid of a half-crown or so, he managed to secure the exclusive use of a first class carriage to Brancaster. He was going to take a decided step, he had thought it all out carefully, and it was shortly after the train had left Cambridge that he turned abruptly to his dusky companion and put a question that startled him.

"Mr. Ramsi," he said, coolly. "Would you mind telling me your real name?"

The other man frowned, but from the way he started, Wendover could see that he had hit the mark.

"I quite fail to understand you," the other said.

"I don't think so," Wendover went on. "Now, mind you, I am not speaking out of idle curiosity. A great deal depends upon whether you are candid with me or not. In the first place, your life is in danger."

Again the Indian started violently.

"Are you threatening me?" he stammered.

"Not at all, my dear sir, not at all. On the contrary, I am your friend, if I can induce you to believe it. I want to help you if I can, and I want you to help me at the same time. For I, also, am connected with the Brotherhood."

As Wendover spoke, he took from his pocket the gold segment and showed it to his companion.

"Unless I am greatly mistaken," he said. "You have a similar section in your pocket. At least, you had the night that we met in Room No. 75 nine months ago."

A queer green shade crept over the Indian's face. He wiped the palms of his hands nervously. Evidently physical courage was not one of his leading virtues.

"In the name of heaven, who are you?" he whispered.

"I have given you my proper name," Wendover went on. "I am the man who asked that night for a sum of money for Miss Corroda. I had no business there, for I am not one of the Brotherhood. On the contrary, I have no sympathy with them whatever. It doesn't matter how I got there, or my motives for being present. I was there, and I recognised you by that nervous upper lip of yours. Oh, yes. I see you have a beard and moustache now, but you weren't wearing it then, neither were you wearing it last night when you lay asleep. No, I didn't burgle your room, I watched you through the ventilator. I dare say you wonder why, and I am going to tell you. Now, I suppose the name of John Garcia is familiar to you?"

The Indian blazed out suddenly.

"Ah, yes," he said. "A cold-blooded and poisonous scoundrel whose one aim and object in life it is to get rid of all of us, and secure the treasure in the safe for himself. It does not matter how I found it out, but I know. And I know that several of us have already fallen before that accursed assassin. And I know that my turn is near at hand. I was denounced because I would not put my hand to crime. My name, sir, is Ran Ghose, and I am a Parsee. I am a man of education, as you see, and all my life I have been mixed up in what you call revolutionary movements. When I came to England, four years ago, for the course of lectures at Cambridge University, I joined the Brotherhood. And would to heaven I had never seen it. Garcia I do not know by sight even, but his hand lies heavy on me now, as it has upon others even more unfortunate than myself. For I have been warned, Mr. Wendover, I have been warned. And that is why I have discarded my Western garb, and gone back to my native dress, and that is why I have assumed my beard and moustache again, although these are false, as you know. And that is why I am going for my little golfing holiday. I ought to be safe at Brancaster. I ought to be happy and comfortable there for a time, at any rate, because I fancy that Garcia does not know me as a Parsee, and that therefore, he can not follow me to the North."

"Ah, that is just where you are mistaken," Wendover said coolly. "I have every reason to believe that your movements are well known to Garcia. He, too, is a master of the art of disguise, and he, too, is probably at Brancaster by this time, staying at the Grand Hotel."

As Wendover spoke, he saw the look of horror in the Parsee's eyes and the moisture oozing on his forehead.

"God help me," he said hopelessly. "But, Mr. Wendover, you are evidently a man of courage, which I am not. If you will help me now, I shall be forever grateful."

"I have come on purpose to help you," Wendover explained. "Perhaps this time I may lay that scoundrel by the heels, though, on two or three occasions he has got the best of me with fatal results to some of your late colleagues. You have to go about, just as if nothing had happened, and, meanwhile, I shall be watching. Do you remember a timid-looking elderly clergyman, who came into the smoking room last night?"

"A little man with grey hair, yes."

"Well, that little man with grey hair was John Garcia. He was watching you, and he was watching me. And comparatively early this morning, with a portmanteau and a bag of golf clubs he set off for Brancaster, where he is staying at the Grand Hotel. And now you realize your danger."

"I am quite in your hands," the Parsee said. "Perhaps we had better turn back."

"And show Garcia that we suspect him," Wendover protested. "Oh, no, we must go through with it now."

XVIII - A FATAL SHOT

It was somewhat early in the season, for it wanted a few weeks before the August rush set in, so that the famous links at Brancaster were not unusually crowded by holiday visitors, though a large number of the usual members were present, together with a handful of enthusiasts staying at the Grand Hotel. A good many of these were personally known to Wendover, as he himself was a fine player, and his presence was hailed with enthusiasm, so that for the next day or two, at any rate, he saw little of Ran Ghose, who, however, was considerably sought after on account of his own record.

It was just as well, Wendover explained, that they should not be seen too often in one another's company, as that would only serve to excite the suspicions of John Garcia, and meanwhile, in his spare time, Wendover was keeping his eyes open. Garcia himself, pottering about in his clerical guise, played golf of a sort. It did not matter much what sort of a performer he was, seeing that there were many elderly gentlemen down there for the benefit of their health, who sauntered round the course from time to time with a club or two, and an experienced caddie, under the delusion they were playing the game. They were harmless old gentlemen for the most part, and a nuisance usually to the general body of players, but these were the crosses that golfers generally had to put up with, especially on such a famous course as Brancaster. So that John Garcia, innocently sporting behind his black coat and white collar, pottered about, no doubt arranging some deep laid scheme for the taking off of the unfortunate Parsee. He always appeared to be in everybody's way, but he was ever ready to apologize and explain that he was no exponent of the game, and that he had taken it up solely on the advice of his medical man.

"You see his game," Wendover said to the Parsee one afternoon, a week or so later, when they had completed an afternoon round and were seated over tea in the smoking-room. "He passes as an amiable old gentleman, always ready to apologise when he gets in anyone's way, and generally treated as a good-tempered nuisance. And, of course, that is all part of the fellow's cunning. He is only waiting his chance."

"But what can he do down here?" Ran Ghose asked. "This is the last place in the world to make an attempt on the life of a fellow creature. It wouldn't be possible on an open golf links like this, and in the hotel it would be out of the question. So many of the golfers sit up half the night playing bridge, there is always someone walking about the corridors."

"Yes, that's all right," Wendover said. "But we have an unusual man to deal with. Garcia undoubtedly has a wonderful imagination, as most of his crimes prove. You may depend upon it, that the attempt will be made here."

The Parsee sighed unhappily, as he rose restlessly from his chair and walked out on the verandah. There his caddie and that of Wendover were waiting with their clubs, hanging round obviously for the usual tip.

"Where did that caddie of yours come from?" Wendover asked. "I thought I knew all the men who caddied in these parts. He looks like a stranger."

"I think he is," Ran Ghose explained. "He has been a sailor, and has not long come back from America. I picked him up the second day I was here, and I have employed him ever since. He is quite a character in his way, very free and independent, but he has picked up a good knowledge of the game somewhere, and he has helped me to win more than one match."

Wendover changed the subject abruptly. After all, it did not much matter, though Wendover had learnt to be cautious and was not disposed to overlook any danger, however remote. He stood there for a moment, looking over the verandah towards the last hole where the players were coming in. Here the course ran parallel with the first two outward holes, and somewhere about a hundred and twenty yards away from the home green was a huge sand dune with a great hollow at its base, which guarded the home green. It was unpleasantly in a line with the first tee, so that a badly pulled ball might carry right across it, and consequently, in fact, prove a source of danger.

"Somebody will get hurt there one of these days," Wendover remarked, as he watched a wild drive from the first tee sail away over the big sand dune. "If a man got in that hazard, and climbed up to the top unexpectedly, he might easily get a blow in the face from one of those practice shots. There, you see what I mean, there are three or four men now, practising driving in front of the first tee, and a carelessly hit ball might do the mischief."

"I dare say," the Parsee said. His mind seemed to be very far away, and his expression was anxious and uneasy. "Are you coming round for a few more holes?"

"I don't think so," Wendover said. "I rather jarred my wrist this afternoon coming home, so I'll give it a rest. I'll just saunter back along the sands."

"Well, I'll take my saddle and practise a few drives," the Parsee said. "You'll say it is cowardly of me, but I feel absolutely safe out there."

He called to his caddie and strode off down the course whilst Wendover made off in the opposite direction, till he came to the sandy margin of the sea, where he sat down quietly to turn matters over in his mind. He was not satisfied with the progress of events. He was puzzled and uneasy, and utterly at a loss to gauge the scheme that Garcia was undoubtedly preparing for the early future.

He had been seated there the best part of an hour when a shout from the links arrested his attention. It was a cry of alarm that brought him suddenly to his feet, and impelled him, almost against his will, in the direction of the club house. Something, undoubtedly, had taken place, and his mind instantly connected it with the Indian. As he looked ahead of him, he could see, on the top of the great sand dune, the spare, ragged figure of Ran Ghose's caddie waving his arms and gesticulating wildly. He was shouting, too, at the top of his voice, but the breeze carried the words away, so that Wendover could make nothing of them. He sprinted across the fairway, and up the slope till he reached the summit of the big mound. He was there first, but the little knot of men who had been practising drives behind the first tee were not far behind, so that they all arrived at the spot more or less simultaneously.

As Wendover looked down into the great hollow beyond he could see the outline of a figure lying there against the white background of sand, could see the turban and the brown face with its fringe of black hair still and set and motionless. And in that moment Wendover knew that the Parsee was dead. In a sudden spasm of rage and disappointment and anger he took the caddie by the arm and whirled him downwards till they both stood there, in the sandy valley, gazing at the unconscious figure lying so motionless here.

"What is it?" Wendover demanded hoarsely. "Stop that infernal row can't you, and tell me what happened."

"It was an accident, sir," the caddie stammered. "I was just coming back with the gentleman, and he drove a ball into here. 'E picked it up and put it in his pocket, then 'e climbed up the face of the bunker to walk down the other side. Just as 'e come to the top he give a funny sort o' cry, then 'e falls right backwards to where 'e is lying, and 'e never moved again. 'E was 'it right in the middle of the forehead by a stray golf ball, an' it's my belief 'e was killed on the spot. Anyway, 'e's dead, sir."

It was even as the dilapidated caddie had said. Ran Ghose lay there in the hollow of sand stone dead. His turban had not been disarranged, not a hair of his moustache and beard was out of place. There was a blue mark in the centre of his forehead with a swelling round it, and as Wendover laid a trembling forefinger upon it, he realized exactly what had happened. The skull had been fractured by the impact to the golf ball, and the man had doubtless died instantly. Beyond question, it was an accident, and this was confirmed a little later on, when one of the white-faced golfers admitted that he had pulled a ball, indeed, more than one over the top of the big hazard, though, so far, there was no sign of the fatal missile. But, anyway, Ran Ghose was dead, and once more with that amazing cleverness of his John Garcia had got the best of the man who had sworn to track him down and bring him to justice.

Wendover followed the body back to the hotel, himself a prey to many conflicting emotions. It seemed almost impossible to get the best of the fiend who had so cunningly planned the series of atrocious murders. And Garcia had covered up his tracks, too, for he was able to prove, a little later on, that he had been in the hotel gardens all the afternoon. He appeared to be just as shocked and horrified as everybody else, but at the same time this alibi of his gave Wendover an idea.

Evidently, for the first time, the man was working with a confederate, for it was impossible that even Garcia could be in two places at once. Wendover walked out across the links in the twilight, deeply pondering over the tragedy. He was going back to the scene of it with some idea of reconstructing what he knew to be a crime.

And there, down in the sandy hollow, stood the strange caddy who had witnessed the accident. His back was towards Wendover, and he appeared to be looking at something in his hand that clinked occasionally as money will do. And there and then Wendover made up his mind. He was going to take a chance, indeed, it was necessary to take a chance to get to the bottom of the suspicion that worried him. He crept on and on until he stood directly behind the figure, then his left hand shot out, and he caught the man with a grip of iron by the nape of the neck, at the same time forcing his head back with his right hand. As he did so, the ragged cap fell from the man's head, and with a closely-cropped wig of rusty brown and dingy fluff that served for hair.

And there below it was an orange-colored flame that Wendover instantly recognised. For the individual in his grasp was the man with the orange-colored hair!

XIX - THE HUT ON THE SANDS

Just for a moment Paul Wendover hesitated and felt half inclined to turn his back on his self-appointed task. He was sick to the very soul of these murderous adventures of his, disappointed and disgusted that he had been powerless to stay the hand of John Garcia. How much longer would they go on, how much longer would it be before he himself was numbered amongst the list of victims? But this was only for a moment, then his hand slipped round to the throat of the man with the orange hair until he was borne gradually backwards and lay on the white and shifting sand with Wendover's knee on his chest. He had put up a big struggle for it, but youth and a magnificent physical training were all on Wendover's side, and, after the first spasmodic effort he had the other entirely at his mercy.

He was afraid of no interruption, either, for the links were deserted now, and down there at the bottom of the crater they were entirely secure from observation.

"Now, you murderous dog," Paul panted. "What have you go to say for yourself?"

The other man choked and gurgled.

"Let me up, can't you," he said, in a strong American accent. "What do you mean by this outrage? You don't look like a common thief, either."

Paul relaxed his grip.

"I'm not," he said. "You can pick up that money and put it back in your pocket. And it's no use you pretending you don't know me, because you do. You have seen me playing golf here often enough. You are the man who carried for Mr. Ramsi. Now, sit up and behave yourself, and answer my questions. What is your name, and where do you come from?"

"No business of yours," the other muttered.

"There you are quite wrong, my friend. It is very much my business. But, first of all, let us understand one another. I am not concerned to know why you, an educated man, are masquerading here as a broken-down golf caddie. What's that? You are a golf caddie? In plain English, that's a lie. To begin with, golf caddies don't wear fine linen like your's, under picturesque rags. Besides, you have not been here very long, and no one knows where you came from. Now, how long have you been in the pay of the man called Garcia?"

The other started, and Paul could see that he had hit the mark.

"I don't know what you mean," came the muttered response.

"Oh, yes, you do. I am going to have an answer if I have to hammer your brains out to get it. How long have you been in the employ of John Garcia? And what did he pay you to murder that unfortunate Parsee?"

Again the orange-haired man started, again his eyes narrowed and his face paled.

"Who the devil are you?" he growled.

"Oh, never mind who I am," Paul said impatiently. "Though as a matter of fact, you know very well. You know that I am Mr. Paul Wendover, and that I came down here with the poor fellow whom you murdered. Yes, I mean it. You killed that man at the instigation of John Garcia, and you are going to tell me why."

"Oh, indeed. Perhaps you know how it was done."

"I do," Paul said curtly. "You have been waiting your chance for days. The whole thing was planned by Garcia, of course, and you merely carried out his instructions. When Mr. Ramsi was down here, looking for his ball, you struck him in the centre of the forehead with some blunt instrument, a blow that fractured his skull, so that he died almost instantly. Then you pretended that he received his injury from a stray golf ball, and everybody believed it, the more especially as there have been several accidents of the kind in the same spot. Now, that is my theory, and if you are not content with it, you can explain to the police, in fact, I will see that you do so. You are not bound to incriminate yourself, but so long as I am your master in strength, I am not going to let you go until I have a proper explanation, that is, unless you prefer to make it to the authorities. When you do, I shall perhaps be able to give my evidence at the same time."

All this was so much bluff on Paul's part, but it had the desired effect. Suddenly the other man's truculent air vanished, and he sat there, trembling from head to foot. Wendover was not slow in pushing his advantage.

"You will gain nothing by your silence," he said. "'I know a great deal more than I have told you. And, once again, I ask you why you did it. Why did you make yourself the tool of that man, Garcia? You are a member of the Brotherhood, the same as he is himself, and it is no part of your duty to become an assassin, merely because he, the head of the Brotherhood, tells you to."

The man with the orange hair started violently.

"What do you know of the Brotherhood?" he demanded.

By way of reply. Paul took the gold disc from his pocket, and held it up before the uneasy eyes of his companion.

"I think that is sufficient proof I know what I am talking about," he said. "And, unless I am greatly mistaken, you have a similar fragment in your pocket at this moment. The last time we met was at the Ambassadors' Hotel about nine months ago. And, since then, many things have happened. Many members of the Brotherhood have fallen; for instance, De Vince and Petroff, and another called Leo Detmar, who was found, though you may not know it, in a corridor at the Ambassadors' Hotel. Now, you may regard all these tragedies as accidents, but I don't. Those men died because John Garcia willed it so, in plain English they were foully murdered by him, so that he might achieve what you are all after."

The red-haired man looked up suddenly.

"Go on," he said hoarsely. "I begin to see daylight. I am beginning to understand things which have puzzled me for a long time. Of course, I knew all these things, we all do, for the matter of that, but I was under the impression that the foreign police had been at work. Do you suggest that I am the tool of John Garcia?"

"I don't suggest anything of the kind," Paul said, coolly. "I know it. He has got tired of slaughter himself, perhaps this succession of crimes has tried even his iron nerve. He may have a suspicion that he is watched, in which he is not far wrong, and that is why he arranged for an alibi. You know what an alibi is, don't you? Yes, of course you do. If anything had gone wrong, he would have been able to shift the blame on you, and go quietly away, rejoicing in the fact that you will hang for this crime, and that another obstacle was removed from his path. Then, unless I am greatly mistaken, the treasure behind the time lock will be his."

The man with the orange hair whistled.

"So that's the game, is it?" he cried. "And I was such a fool that I never suspected it. Now, see here, mister, I am entirely in your hands, the game has gone wrong, and you can hang me if you like. I came here prepared to take the risk, and I would do it again, but I don't want to find myself dancing at the end of a rope till I have got even with John Garcia. You see, it's like this, I have been a member of the Brotherhood for years. I used to live in Scotland at one time before I emigrated to the States with my wife and child. I was a happy and industrious engineer then, with what looked like a fine future before me. I dare say if I had stayed in Scotland all would have been well, but I was an ambitious chap, and Europe wasn't big enough for me. So I went to America, and it was the worst day's work I ever did in my life. I was robbed of two or three inventions, then I got mixed up in a big strike and, through no fault of my own, found myself in gaol. When I came out again my wife was dead, and so was the child. They had been starved to death whilst I was being punished for a crime that I never committed. And that made a devil of me. From that moment my hand was against everybody's. I hated everyone who was better off than myself. Then I got into the Brotherhood, and I have been one of the big men in it ever since. I have been ready for everything. I was prepared to commit murder on the least provocation. I hated all capitalists, and I hated the man in the street, who toadied to and flattered him."

As the man with the orange-colored hair went on his eyes gleamed, and he beat the air with his fists like one who is almost beside himself. For here was the true fanatic, the so-called social martyr who is ready to give up his life for the cause; an anarchist, ready made and prepared to wade through blood to gain his end. Wendover watched him with curiosity, and saw how deeply moved he was and encouraged him.

"I think I understand," he said. "As a matter of fact, you are just the sort of man Garcia wanted for his purpose. But what had the unfortunate Parsee done?"

"Betrayed the cause, or so I was told. Refused to carry out one of their mandates. Declined to carry out a commission and fled to England. Here he changed his name and assumed his native dress, and only attended our meetings disguised in his mask so that he could get information that he could use for his own safety. But Garcia found out. Garcia tracked him down and followed him here. Then I came on the scene. It is getting a little chilly here, don't you think if you will come with me as far as my hut, I will go on with my story."

"Where is this place?" Wendover asked.

"The ruined coastguard station on the edge of the beach. I have got a few sticks and two rooms there, and nobody interferes with me. They look upon me as a wandering golf caddie who is perfectly harmless, and as there are none too many caddies they don't worry me."

"Lead the way," Wendover said curtly.

They came presently to the melancholy ruin that stood just above high water mark amongst the lonely sand dunes on the far side of the course. Here was a broken table and chair, and an apology for a bed in one corner.

"Why do you stay here?" Wendover asked.

"Because my task is not finished," the other said.

Wendover looked sharply into the face of his companion. There was something almost sinister in the suggestion.

"What do you mean by that?" he asked.

"Well, I don't know; but I believe that there is someone else. Garcia is not the man to tell people much, but I am told to wait instructions. Still, as far as I can gather, the Parsee was not the only traitor."

"Traitor," Wendover scoffed. "That is what you call them, is it? Anybody would think that Garcia and his murderous gang represented some State bent upon punishing some one guilty of treason. I tell you, my friend, that the Parsee was a harmless individual, a dreamer of dreams, who lived and died under the delusion that he was born to set the world straight. And I tell you that Garcia deliberately trapped Ramsi. He wanted the Indian out of the way, the same as he wants you out of the way."

"I am beginning to believe that he does," the man with the orange-colored hair said thoughtfully. "Mister, it's rather a pity we didn't meet before."

"It is," Wendover said. "I should have saved you from a cold-blooded murder if I had."

The other looked up with a challenge in his eyes.

"Here, drop that," he said. "But I don't know, perhaps you are right in what you think. Do you believe that it was I who killed the nigger?"

"I have already told you so," Wendover said.

"Well, I didn't. You've got it all wrong. I came up here, because Garcia sent for me. He sent me the sign that I dare not disobey. Not that I knew it was Garcia till I got here. But why did he send for me? He sent for me, because he knew that I had been an enthusiastic golfer in my youth, and because he wanted me to pose as a caddie here. Well, that was easy enough, as you know, but he didn't tell me any more, not till the day of the Parsee's death. He's not that sort of man. I'm not sure yet that it is Garcia that I am dealing with, though I have been pretty sure in my mind all along. You see, it's like this: He came to me here and reminded me of my oath to the Brotherhood, the oath of implicit obedience to every order that comes from Headquarters. And, because I thought the man was a traitor, I obeyed. A man like me who has his hand against everybody—"

The speaker trailed off into a wild tirade of abuse against humanity generally, and the old insane gleam was dancing in his eyes again. Wendover pulled him up sharply.

"Never mind about that just now," he commanded.

"Beg your pardon, mister. I always go off like that when I begin think of my wrongs. I was to lure the Parsee into that big sand bunker on the first opportunity when those players came out to practise their tee shots after tea. And I did it, as you know. As we were coming back, I suggested to the Indian that he should try and carry that big bunker from an impossible distance, and he tried it. It didn't come off, as I knew, but the ball trickled into the bunker instead. And when we came up with it, Garcia was lurking there, hidden from sight with a lasso in his hand. Garcia is a South American, and he can do anything with a lasso. And what do you think he did? He threw the noose weighted with lead at either end and struck the nigger on the forehead. He did it deliberately, of course, with the intention of killing the man, and he did. He knew exactly what was going to happen, and he was not far wrong. The Indian dropped like a stone and was dead in a second. Then I raised a cry, and Garcia slipped off unseen by anybody. And that's the way we got rid of a traitor. But I had no hand in it, mister, except to cover Garcia's tracks, and I give you my word, I hadn't the least notion what was going to happen until the whole thing was over. Not that it would have made much difference if I had. Because, you see, the man is a traitor, and I have suffered enough at the hands of that class. I tell you that my wife and child—"

The speaker threw up his hands again and began to rave and shout like one beside himself.

"Will you drop it?" Wendover commanded. "Man alive, can't you see the peril you stand in? Don't you know that in the eyes of the law you are as guilty of this crime as Garcia is himself. You would be hanged without mercy if I only spoke the word. But you are, apparently, only a mere tool in this business, and I don't want to be too hard on you. Now, listen to me. You have been made use of in the same way as you were when in America. You are the class of man who always pulls the chestnuts of the cunning scoundrels who play for their own ends. And this is what you are doing now for John Garcia. You are his mere puppet. Why? Because he has one object in life only, and that is to gain possession of the money in that safe. He has already got several of the Brotherhood out of the way, and now that you have served his purpose your turn is at hand, as sure as the sun rises on the morrow. When you are all dead, and there are no witnesses left, which will be before the next meeting of the Brotherhood, Garcia will turn up in that mysterious room alone and fill his pockets with the contents of the safe. And now you understand what is going on?"

The other man rubbed his eyes as if he were slowly coming to consciousness after a long sleep.

"I begin to see, mister," he said. "Yes, I believe you are right. But, see here; where do you come in? My instructions tell me that there is another traitor in the way yet. Do you know who he is?"

Wendover started suddenly. This was a new light to him, but it was getting plainer every moment.

"Why, I am," he exclaimed. "I was a fool that I didn't see it before. So it is part of your duty to get me out of the way as well as the Parsee. And you are the instrument who is going to help to do it. Well, forewarned is forearmed. Now, doesn't it occur to you that your turn is coming as well? Are you going to submit blindly to be treated in this fashion, or are you going to join hands with me, and help to bring Garcia to justice. Do you believe that man's story or mine?"

"I am with you," the orange-haired man said hoarsely. "I'm with you, mister, all the time. It puzzles me how an English gentleman, like yourself, has got mixed up with this business, and how you found out all about it."

"Never mind that," Wendover said. "I went amongst that nest of criminals to see justice done. But you were there on the last meeting of the Brotherhood. I recognise you by the color of your hair. You were there just opposite me. I am the man who brought Miss Corroda's case before the Brotherhood, and I it was who obtained that money for her. She has been most infamously treated."

"That's right," the other man said. "And I'll help you, as far as she's concerned, with pleasure. I met old man Corroda in the States some years ago, before he made all that money, and he was very kind to me. And if I hadn't been a fool, I should have seen what was going on. But, in my eyes, the Brotherhood was a sacred thing, a band of genuine patriots gathered together to right wrongs all over the world. And when all that money came along, it seemed to me that there was nothing to stop us. But I see differently now. What do you want me to do, mister. How can I help?"

"Tell me your right name first," Wendover asked.

"Well, call me Jabez Martin. That will do as well as any other, and besides, it happens to be my right name. And now, what's the next move, Mr. Wendover?"

Paul would have given a good deal to have been able to say. Had he acted on the impulse of the moment, he would have gone straight away from there and denounced Garcia to the police. But, for the moment, at any rate, there was nothing to be gained by that. To begin with, the authorities would have demanded something in the way of proof, and that, for the present, he was not in a position to give them. He could only wait and watch, and hope for the best. He could only keep his eyes open and guard against the coming tragedy as far as he was concerned. And any day the blow might fall.

"I confess," he said, "that I hardly venture to strike again till some days have elapsed. Therefore you had better go on as if nothing had happened, behave as if you had not seen me, and gain all the information you can. Meanwhile, you can assume your disguise again, and keep up the role of a golf caddie. And if I want to see you, I can easily run across from the hotel here. And if you want to speak to me, you will have plenty of opportunities of doing so. But don't forget that we have a tiger to deal with."

Wendover turned away and made his way slowly along the sand dunes in the direction of the hotel. Coming towards him in the distance, was a figure that was familiar to him, the well-known outline of Garcia, in his clerical garb, carrying what apparently appeared to be a butterfly net with a specimen case slung over his shoulder.

Wendover dropped behind a clump of long grass and lay there till Garcia was almost upon him. From time to time the latter darted ahead as if in eager quest of specimens, then he paused and looked furtively around him. There was an evil grin on those thin lips of his, and a lurid light in his cunning eyes. Apparently he was bent on some mischievous errand, working towards his quarry slowly and cautiously, as if fearful that someone might be watching him from the hotel through a pair of glasses. And so, by slow degrees, he worked his way along the sand dunes till he came to the ruined house, in front of which he stood for a moment, and then slowly entered.

Wendover rose to his feet, and retraced his footsteps. If there was anything serious taking place within the hut then most assuredly he would be there to see.

XXI - THE QUARREL

The light was still fairly strong, so that it was possible for Wendover to see what was going on inside the room. Taking advantage of the scrub outside, he crept on his hands and knees near enough to get a view of the open door and the dingy room beyond. He could see that Martin was seated there with his head in his hands, lost to his surroundings, and evidently plunged into deep thought. He looked up in a dull, uncomprehending way as Garcia came forward, then something like fear and loathing crept into his eyes, and he rose to his feet.

"What are you doing here?" he demanded. "What do you want? Haven't I done enough for you? It's all very well for you to have the command of money to get about from place to place, but what of me? You know that I am penniless, you know that I had to walk part of the way here, and you have seen to it that I have to live on the few shillings I earn. And you promised me when the business of the Parsee was finished that you would give me money and let me go."

"Presently, presently," Garcia said soothingly. "But your work is not yet finished. I told you there was much yet to be done. And what are you doing like that? Where is your cap, and what has become of your wig? Are you mad that you go about like this? If anyone were to see you now all sorts of suspicions might be set on foot. You are a wandering golf caddie, remember; a broken-down man who gets a precarious living by doing odd jobs. Don't you understand that?"

"Oh, I understand that," Martin said sullenly. "Perhaps I understand more than you give me credit for."

A sudden anger flamed into Garcia's eyes. His thin lips compressed like a steel trap.

"Don't you threaten me!" he said. "'And don't you dare to run counter to the wishes of the Brotherhood. Remember that you are here on duty. You have instructions that must be carried out to the letter, or you will take the consequences, and I need not point out what those consequences are. The man who disobeys instructions from headquarters is a traitor, just as much as the Parsee was, and he suffers accordingly. Now sit down again and listen to me."

Martin dropped suddenly into his seat

"Go on," he muttered. "Go on. John Garcia-that is, if your name is John Garcia.

"My name," the other said sternly, "to most people, is the Reverend James Ogilvy. I am a harmless old scientist, who plays golf for the benefit of his health, and collects butterflies as a hobby. But I am John Garcia, and the head of the Brotherhood, and all who belong to it must obey my slightest word. You have had your instructions under the seal of the Brotherhood, and they must be carried out to the letter. You have already seen what it means to disobey."

"I have seen a man foully murdered if that is what you mean," Martin retorted. "But he was a harmless chap, that Parsee, and if I liked to speak—"

"Well, speak then. Go and denounce me to the police. Tell them the story of what happened in the great sand bunker. Go and do it now, and I won't put up my hand a yard to stop you. Tell them who John Garcia is. Oh, pooh you fool: John Garcia laughs at the police-he has been laughing at them for years. They will never lay their hand upon him. They think, even at the present moment, that he is in prison in Geneva."

"I thought so, too," Martin muttered.

"Well, then, he isn't. Look here!"

As Garcia spoke, he took the clerical hat from his head, and removed his spectacles. It was only a little thing but it altered him almost beyond recognition. The cruel little eyes were full of menace, the thin lips were drawn in a straight line, and Martin suddenly weakened.

"I am John Garcia," the man said. "Cast your mind back to a few months ago, to the last meeting of the Brotherhood. You were there, and heard all that happened, you were told that John Garcia was in gaol, and that the man who represented him had in his possession proofs of the treacherous interference of a certain outsider. You saw those proofs put in the safe. They were put in the safe for me, John Garcia himself, because I, for my part, did not want even the Brotherhood to know that my place in prison had been taken by a trusty comrade—"

"Leo Detmar," Martin blurted out.

Garcia's eyes gleamed angrily.

"Oh, so you know that much, do you," he said. "Not that it very much matters. Now, Leo Detmar is dead—"

"Murdered," Martin cried. "Murdered."

"Oh, so you know that, too. Well, perhaps you shall help me to avenge him some day. But before that happens I have a score to settle with the man who betrayed me to the Geneva police. And you are going to help me."

"Oh, I am, am I?"

"Yes, you are. Now that man was present at the meeting of the Brotherhood, masked like the rest of us, with his credentials in his pocket, though how he got there and where he obtained those credentials from puzzles even me. Still, he was there, and I know his name. He is an English journalist called Paul Wendover. He is staying here at the present moment. You know him as well as I do."

"I do," Martin muttered. "What of him?"

"What of him? That is my most dangerous and implacable enemy. He has made it his business to thwart and oppose me at every possible turn. He has been in contact with me over and over again without knowing it; indeed, he has not the least idea who the Reverend James Ogilvy really is. But he will find out to his cost before long. He'll be sorry that he ever interfered with me. He'll be sorry that he ever met Zena Corroda, and made it his special business to restore her fortune to her. That man is the most dangerous enemy the Brotherhood has. He has got to be removed."

"And I am to help, I suppose?" Martin asked. "Well, I decline to do anything of the sort. No more bloodshed for me; do your dirty work yourself."

"Then you refuse?"

"Then I refuse. What do I care what happens to me? I am almost a starving man, without a friend in the world, and he who puts a bullet through me is doing me a real kindness. Besides, I have met the man you speak of and I like him. He is an honest and straightforward English gentleman, and I am sure he would befriend me if I told him everything. Therefore, John Garcia you can go to hell and do your work in your own way. I defy you."

Martin sprang to his feet, and stood facing Garcia, with his eyes blazing and a look of determination on his face. Just for an instant it appeared to the watcher as if the men were about to fly at one another's throats. Then, apparently Garcia thought the better of it, for he laughed irritably, and dropped to his seat again.

"Very well," he said. "If you won't help me, I can't force you. But do you know what the consequences are? I shall have to report you to the Brotherhood."

"You can't do it," Martin laughed defiantly. "You can't do it, because there are none of the Brotherhood left. They are all dead, except yourself. They have all been murdered, or hanged, or otherwise got rid of—"

"Got rid of by me?" Garcia demanded.

"I didn't say that, I said they had been got rid of. And so they have. We are the two remaining ones, and I don't count. And perhaps I also shall be beyond trouble before the next annual meeting takes place. And if I am, then it will be a fine thing for you."

"What do you mean by that?" Garcia demanded.

"Oh, well," Martin laughed scornfully. "I think you know what I mean. There is a fine fortune waiting in that safe for the last lucky survivor of the Brotherhood. A fortune that could be devoted, no doubt, to furthering our aims. And, on the other hand, you mightn't do anything of the sort. You might decide to keep it yourself, and live happy and comfortable ever afterwards."

Garcia listened with an indifferent expression on his face. He snarled, as a man does who listens with toleration to the weaknesses of other people. But Wendover had a pretty fair idea of what was passing through his mind. It was no part of his scheme just now to drive the orange-colored haired man any further. When he spoke again it was quite mildly.

"I am sorry to hear you talk like that," he said. "Because you are doing me a great injustice. And, after all, it is just possible that you may be the sole survivor. However, this is all wasting time. If you won't help me, you won't, and there's an end of it. But there's one little thing I should like you to do for me before I leave here to-morrow. Do you know that big house, standing in its own grounds about three miles inland on the far side of the links? You do, of course. Well, that house belongs to a famous oculist, who comes down here to play golf. What's that? You've seen him. Very well, then I may tell you that a friend of mine is going to call upon him to-morrow afternoon by appointment, with a view to having his eyes tested. He will come back across the golf links to the hotel, where a note from me awaits him, and I want you to show him the way. If you will stand out there on the dunes at that time, you will see him come in your direction, and will offer to show him the way. He is very short-sighted, and you will recognise him by his blue glasses. No, it doesn't matter about his name. All you have to do is to take him to the hotel, never mind why. He is one of us, and that is sufficient reason for you."

"Oh, I'll do that," Martin said. "But that's the last. Then I think I shall get away myself."

Wendover rose to his feet and made his way cautiously towards the hotel. He had found out a good deal. He was satisfied that he was safe for the present, and he made up his mind that he could not trust either of these men. Still, there was something in the wind, and he would not be far off to-morrow afternoon when Martin met the stranger with the blue glasses.

XXII - A LONG SHOT

The Reverend James Ogilvy wandered about the smoking-room of the Grand Hotel, talking golf with one visitor or another, as if he were really what he pretended to be —a kindhearted, amiable, old nuisance, who played golf for the sake of his health, and devoted all the rest of innocent life to the collection of butterflies. He seemed to go almost out of his way to make himself agreeable to Wendover, who deemed it prudent to accept these advances in a friendly spirit. It was not for him to give Garcia the slightest clue that his real identity had been disclosed. So they sat side by side in the smoking-room, as if they had been friends of years' standing.

"Are you really going to-morrow?" Wendover asked.

"I am sorry to say I am," the other bleated. "I have had a most enjoyable time in this wonderful air, and my golfing holiday has done me a world of good. Not that I shall ever be a player, Mr. Wendover, no. And I dare say most of you players have found me a great nuisance, but you will make allowances for a very old man, whose one regret it is that he has taken up the game too late in life."

It was all so naturally done that Wendover could not fail to admire it. For that murderous rascal was the innocent country clergyman to the life, and, no doubt, he was inwardly chuckling to himself at the success of his pose. And yet, under that placid exterior was the heart of a tiger and the tenacity of a ferret. Still, his eyes were smiling as he beamed benignly on the assembled golfers.

"Yes, I am going to-morrow," he said. "But I hope to come here again before long. I should not go now, had I not urgent business in the north."

"You go by the afternoon train?" Wendover asked.

"Oh, no. I go in a little car of mine. It comes for me here just after lunch. I drive it myself; perhaps a stupid thing to do at my time of life, but I am very careful, and never exceed twenty miles an hour. Besides, a friend of mine is being brought here in the car to see Dr. Smart, the great eye specialist, who has kindly offered to give him an hour or two to-morrow afternoon. Then my friend comes on here to stay for a day or two in my place. He is nearly blind, so he will need to be brought here. I have arranged for one of the golf caddies to meet him and bring him here, and perhaps, Mr. Wendover, you will be so kind as to take him for a little walk occasionally."

Wendover muttered something to the effect that he would be delighted. But, in the back of his mind, he was wondering what all this was leading to, and what cunning scheme Garcia was working out. He did not believe for a moment that that rascal was in the least interested in any patient of Dr. Smart, so that he did not even trouble to ask the name of the newcomer. He would be near enough tomorrow afternoon when the stranger came along, in company with Martin, and it would go hard if he did not find out for himself.

"That's very good of you, Mr. Wendover," Garcia said. "And now, I wish you good night and good-bye. As I have a fairly long journey before me to-morrow, I must go to bed early. I hope that we shall meet again."

The last words dropped from Garcia's lips with what seemed to Wendover like a ring of menace in them. But it was no part of his policy to notice this, and perhaps, after all, it was only fancy.

He was down early in the morning, only to find that Garcia's little car had come along, and that the Reverend James Ogilvy had departed in the direction of the North Road. But he could not ascertain that anybody came in the car, which had been brought from a neighboring garage, nor when he saw the famous oculist on the links later on in the morning could he ascertain by a few guarded enquiries that the latter was expecting to see a patient. This discovery rather startled Wendover, and left him a little more puzzled than ever. He finished his morning round, and presently lunched alone in the Club House. For the next hour or two, he wandered about the links, trying, more or less vainly, to fit the pieces of the puzzle together, then, a little before four o'clock, he went back to the hotel to get out his motor cycle. He invariably took this with him on golfing holidays, with a view to an occasional visit to some distant links, for there were many of these along the north-east coast, and most of them were well known to him.

To get to the top of the golf links on his Indian machine he had to make a rather wide detour of some four or five miles before he struck the sand dunes again, and it was past four o'clock before he wheeled the machine into a clump of bushes and sat down in a sandy hollow to smoke a cigarette and wait upon events. From where he was seated he had a full view of the large house which was occupied by Dr. Smart, and which lay a mile or so ahead of him, so that he was tolerably sure of the fact that no one could reach or leave the house without his knowing it. It was very lonely and quiet there, nothing but a succession of little sand hills, stretching along an arm of the bay, with the wide expanse of flat country beyond. There was no road here, nothing but an occasional sheep track, and, at this time of the year, most of the flocks had been driven further inland, so that, but for an occasional sea bird, and a rabbit or two, Wendover had the whole landscape to himself. For a long time he sat there, thinking things over, wondering when this tangle of blood and slaughter was going to finish, and when he would be free from the danger that for months now had been hanging over him day and night. He was getting impatient, too, for the delay and the solitude of that lonely spot were pressing on his nerves, and he was longing for the moment of action to arrive.

Then, presently, it seemed to him that he could see some dark object moving along the main road about a mile or two away. A little later, the object resolved itself into a car, which, apparently, was being driven by one man, though it was too far away for Wendover to make sure of the point, and he was annoyed with himself because he had forgotten to bring a pair of glasses with him. If he had had the foresight to do so, he would have been able to distinguish the driver of the car. Then the car pulled up, apparently under the wall that ran round the big house, and the driver got out. He was lost to sight for a little while, no doubt he had passed through the gateway into the grounds. And then as Wendover turned to glance behind, and make sure that he was still alone, he thrilled as he saw something moving amongst the sand dunes about a hundred yards to the left. But he smiled to himself a moment later as he made out the outline of the man with the orange-colored hair.

"Upon my word, my nerves are playing all sorts of tricks with me this afternoon," Wendover muttered. "Of course, Martin will be there. He's there on purpose. And here am I trying to hide myself, forgetting all the time that he will be close at hand. I wonder if he has spotted me?"

But evidently the man with the orange-colored hair had not noticed Wendover, for he sat there, on the top of a heap of sand, with his face turned in the direction of the Doctor's house. Wendover crouched a little lower.

"I'll not let him know I am here," he decided to himself. "After all, he doesn't know what I heard yesterday when I was lying outside the hut, and there is no reason why I should trust any of these people any further than is necessary. It's just likely, too, that I've come on a fool's errand. It is possible, after all, that Garcia really has got a short-sighted friend who wants to consult the doctor. It is possible too, that Martin might have changed his mind, in which case he and Garcia will have a fine chance of getting rid of me, if they discover me in this lonely spot. Therefore, I think I'll just lie low, and play Brer Rabbit."

He carefully extinguished his cigarette, and made himself as inconspicuous as possible, lying so close that he could observe everything going on about him without being seen himself. He could see Martin plainly enough, and all across the intervening sand dunes to the spot where the motor car was standing. Then, presently, a figure emerged from the doctor's house, and came slowly and hesitatingly along the road till it suddenly branched towards the links. It was some fifteen hundred yards away from where Wendover was now, plainly picked out in the strong sunlight, and, so far as Wendover could make out, the figure carried a long walking stick in his hands. As the man with the flame-colored hair caught sight of it he moved forward in the direction of the new-comer. Then the stranger seemed to stand still for a moment, as if undecided what to do next. He carried his stick in his hands, crosswise, then stood with shoulders hunched and feet apart. Wendover broke out into a sudden cry. But it was too late, for he could see a tiny puff of smoke, followed by a noise no louder than the crack of a whip, and at the same instant Martin threw up his hands and fell face downward in the sand without a sound.

He had been shot through the heart; he lay there stone dead, as Wendover knew before he could wriggle across the intervening sand on his hands and knees. In the course of his adventures he had seen a man die before, and he knew those symptoms only too well.

Martin lay there, stone dead; he must have died instantly. Just for a moment Wendover hesitated as to what to do next. Should he go back to the hotel and give the alarm, or should he clear out without saying a word to anyone? A moment later this question was decided for him, for the man who fired the shot had climbed into the car, and was now fast receding into the distance.

A sudden light broke on Wendover.

"By Heavens," he cried. "That is Garcia's car, and Garcia himself. He has got Martin out of the way, and he would have had me out of the way, too, by this time if yonder poor fellow had not defied him. I'll follow him up; I'll track him down, and put an end to this once and for all."

The coast was clear now, so that Wendover raced across to where his motor bike was hidden, and mounted without delay. He could cover his fifty or sixty miles an hour easily; he would be on the track of the car before it had gone many miles. He had only the clothes he stood up in, and a few pounds in his pocket, but he was not thinking of that so much as vengeance.

XXIII - A STERN CHASE

The blood was pounding in Wendover's head, and the red light was in his eyes as he moved along in the direction of the car. Just for the moment all prudence had gone to the winds, and if he had come up with Garcia at that particular moment then indeed it would have gone ill with that murderous foreigner. For Wendover was tired and weary of all this slaughter, so much so that he longed to be in some foreign country, where the arm of the law is not so long, so that he might have taken matters in his own hands and ended Garcia's career once and for all.

It was only for a moment or two, and then he was himself again. He set his 'Indian' going, and sped swiftly along the smooth road in the direction of the car which he knew, beyond the shadow of a doubt, held the man who was responsible for all this shedding of blood. He knew, too, that, given ordinary conditions, he would be up alongside Garcia within the course of half-an-hour, because the car in front was a small, two-seater affair, and the 'Indian' motor cycle was capable of anything up to eighty miles an hour. Moreover, the country was quiet in this part, with little or no traffic on the road, so that there was no danger so far as the public were concerned, and no probability of police traps whatever. And again, pursuit was the last thing Garcia would be expecting. No doubt he was hugging himself with the delusion that his carefully-laid plans had been entirely successful, and that no one had seen the fatal shot fired. Probably Garcia's first idea had been to get rid of both his enemies at the same time, but apparently he had abandoned that part of the programme, when he had discovered that Martin was not so amenable to reason as he had expected. Therefore, he would probably go quietly along the road to Hull, or some such big seaport town, where he would be lost to view for the moment, and where he could sit quietly down and plan the destruction of the last life that stood between him and the treasure in Room No. 75.

If Wendover had been a little less carried away by his feelings, he would probably have contented himself with following Garcia at a reasonable distance, and quietly making sure of his whereabouts for making the next move. But the swift motion through the air, and the rushing speed of his 'Indian,' did nothing to smooth down his anger. He sped on mile after mile, utterly reckless as to the future. It had not occurred to him, either that the silent way in which he disappeared from the Grand Hotel might cause enquiries to be made, and perhaps some suspicious individual might connect him with the body of the golf caddie, which must be found before long, lying there, on the sands. But all this, Wendover decided, would keep. He trusted to his native talent to get him out of that.

Then, presently, as he swept suddenly round a curve, he almost ran into the car that was jogging quietly along the road in front of him. It was too late to turn back, too late to try and hide himself, for Garcia glanced over his shoulder and the eyes of the two men met. And in those of Garcia Wendover could see a look of absolute fear. It was fear that gleamed behind those spectacles, and it was a very white and ghastly face that showed under the clerical hat. Evidently Wendover was beginning to get upon his enemy's nerves, evidently the man was beginning to feel that here was a force he could not shake off. He accelerated his speed, and shot ahead just a little and then it seemed to Wendover that the man he was after was throwing something out of the back of the car.

He found himself speculating idly as to what it was, but he was to know only too soon. A second later there was a sound of a quick report, and the 'Indian' slowed up suddenly with a big puncture in the front tyre.

There was no help for it, and Wendover cursed aloud as he dismounted and surveyed the damage, which meant a delay of at least an hour. He might have known, he told himself, that the cunning scoundrel in front of him would be prepared for every emergency of the kind. Then he set himself doggedly down to make good the mischief which took him rather longer than he anticipated, and then he pushed on again to pick up the tracks of the man in front of him. But this was a slow and tedious process, and it was nearly 10 o'clock before he rode into Hull, and with the aid of a friendly policeman or two located the man he was after in the Queen's

Hotel. He put up here himself at a smaller house, and called for the meal which he so badly needed. Then he sat down to a cigar and a cup of coffee to think out his position.

All he had was a pound of two in his pocket and the grey flannel suit that he stood up in. His first business was to call up the proprietor of the Grand Hotel at Brancaster.

"It's Mr. Wendover speaking," he said. "That you, Mr. Jackson? Oh, yes, I came along this afternoon for a spin on my motor-cycle, and went further than I intended. I had a bad breakdown on the way, and decided to push on to Hull. I am here, at the King's Hotel, and I may have to stay a day or two because my machine has been rather badly damaged, and I think I shall wait until it is repaired. What's that? Oh, yes, please send on my portmanteau and odds and ends the first thing in the morning. Shall you keep my room? Well, no, I don't think so, you see, I may be detained here longer than I expect, and I'll take my chance. My kind regards to all my friends there, and I hope they are well. Nothing out of the common happened, I suppose? No fresh records established, eh?"

The reply of the hotel proprietor was re-assuring—nothing had happened, and evidently no tragic discovery had been made, or he would have said so. With an easier mind, Wendover attacked the telephone again, and called up the editor of the 'Daily Herald' in London, whom he got in a quarter of an hour, it was a somewhat long message, but it was through at length, and Wendover retired to bed with the assurance that the necessary funds were on their way.

Early next morning he made cautious inquiries at the Queen's Hotel, where an unexpected check awaited him. The clerk in the office perfectly remembered the clergyman who had come there the day before in a little two-seater car, and who had signed the visitors book in the name of James Ogilvy. He was no longer in the hotel, apparently he had put up his car in some neighboring garage, and, after breakfast had paid his bill, and had gone off in the direction of the docks in a taxi. At the end of an hour Wendover had ascertained that the man he was in search of had booked a passage for Norway, and had dropped out of the docks in a Norwegian steamer about eleven o'clock that morning. He had evidently gone on a fishing excursion, for he had taken a number of rods, and such-like baggage with him. It was quite an unexpected rebuff, and it left Wendover utterly bewildered for the moment.

Angry and disappointed, he went back to his hotel there to sit down quietly in the smoking-room and ponder over what was best to be done next. Obviously, Garcia was merely covering his tracks. That he had gone to Norway for any length of time Wendover declined to believe. He would be back again before long, no doubt, in another disguise, ready to take up the business where he had dropped it. For the time had come now when only one life stood between him and the treasure in the safe, and when he did strike he would strike swiftly and without mercy. It was unfortunate that he had slipped away just at this time, for Wendover had felt comparatively safe so long as his enemy was more or less in sight.

He was still pondering this over when a stranger in a grey lounge suit entered the smoking-room and accosted Wendover by name.

"What on earth are you doing here?" the newcomer asked. "Up to some of your old games, eh. Still playing the amateur detective on behalf of that paper of yours. Do you remember that business you dragged me into at Vienna?"

"Why, bless my soul, it's Walton," Wendover cried. "I had quite forgotten you lived in Hull. And I suppose you had quite forgotten we were going to have a little golf together at St. Andrews this autumn. Or was it some late salmon fishing? Upon my word, I forget."

"Fishing," the man called Walton said. "I haven't forgotten it; in fact, I was going to write to you to-morrow. But, unfortunately, I can't get away. My partner is laid up, and until he comes back to business I am tied by the leg. And there is some of the best fishing in the north of Scotland spoiling, and here am I chained to the docks. But why shouldn't you go? Got no tackle here? What on earth's that got to do with it? Come round to my place, and I'll fit you out in half an hour. You go on up there for a few days, and I'll try and snatch a long week-end, anyhow. You'll have it all to yourself, with the exception of a queer old Johnnie that the Guv-nor scraped acquaintance with and gave an invitation to. But I don't even know that he's gone there yet. In fact, he called at the office when I was out this morning, and left a message to the effect that he was running over to Norway on business."

Wendover looked up swiftly.

"What's the old man's name?" he asked carelessly.

"Ogilvy. The Rev. James Ogilvy. My old father's a bit of a naturalist, as you know, and he is always scraping acquaintances with some old bore or another. And you know how good-natured he is. Doesn't fish himself, but always ready to find a rod for somebody else. Still, it doesn't much matter, and the reverend gentleman has gone to Norway, though he does hope to come back at the end of next week. But never mind about him. Will you go up to South Glen?"

Wendover's friend little realized how eagerly the latter jumped at the opportunity. It was as if fate had conspired to throw Garcia into his way again, and that Garcia would come back he felt sure. And he felt sure, too, that that murderous ruffian had merely crossed over to Norway in order to cover his tracks.

"Oh, I'll go up to South Glen, right enough," he said. "I'll go up to-morrow. Not that I shall catch any fish till this weather changes. It's too dry for anything."

XXIV - ON THE RIVER

Everything being arranged, and Wendover feeling easier in his mind now, all he had to do was to kill time until the arrival of his traps, and, when they came, make his way to Scotland with a sure and certain feeling that he would see Garcia again before long. And for the first time since he had set out upon his self-appointed task, luck appeared to be on his side, and, indeed, his meeting with Cecil Walton had been luck, pure and simple. By some fortunate chance Garcia had come in contact with Walton's kind-hearted, good-natured father, and the invitation to try a few days' salmon fishing had followed as a matter of course. And very probably Garcia had jumped at it. For Wendover knew him to be a good deal of a sportsman, and, besides, the wily South American would probably be glad of a few quiet days in that remote part of the world, when he could kill a salmon or two and brood over his plans for the future at the same time. And now the opportunity had come, just at the moment when he wanted it. He would be back from Norway in a week, and would proceed to that quiet, sporting retreat without the least idea that he was going to run straight into the arms of the last man in the world that he wanted to see.

Wendover chuckled when he thought of it. He would meet Garcia alone with the possible exception of the keeper, they would be fishing a stream together, and Garcia, of course, would recognise him. But would Garcia come back in the guise of the Rev. James Ogilvy, or would he adopt some other character? Wendover decided that he would come back as the Rev. James Ogilvy, and when he discovered who his companion was, would bluff the thing out. But this, of course, was a matter of pure speculation. There was only one thing to do, to wait and see what was on the lap of the future.

It was intensely hot. It had been a long and fiery summer, and the whole country was dried and parched and burned up. The British Isles had not known such a drought for the last century. For the moment, at any rate, fishing was out of the question, though directly the rain came, and it could not be long delayed now, the rivers would be full again, and doubtless there would be a fine run of autumn fish straight from the sea. And besides, there were trout to think of, and the South Glen trout fishing was some of the best in the world.

On the third day, Wendover turned his back on the sweltering seaport town, and made his way to Scotland. It was the same all along the route everywhere, the same tale of drought with the fields burned brown, and the leaves on the trees like burnished copper. The streams had dwindled down till they were no more than silver threads between their banks, and the old keeper on the South Glen estate turned a serious face to Wendover as he related his tale of woe of shrunken streams and empty creel.

"It's no use I'll be to you, Mr. Wendover," he said. "At least, not till the rains come. Maybe you'll get a trout or two, but you'll not want me for that."

So, for a day or two Wendover wandered along the stream, getting an occasional trout from a pool here and there, and meanwhile wondering as to whether or not he was wasting his time. And yet he could do nothing except idle the burning days away, writing most days to Zena, who was still somewhere holiday making on the south coast. More than once he was inclined to pack his bag and go and join her till such time as it was possible to strike again. And then all that dogged resolution came back to him, that grim determination not to turn for a moment from the task before him until it was finished, and he had that arch-fiend Garcia at his mercy.

It was too hot to do anything, almost too hot to think. Each morning the sun rose in a sky of copper and poured down mercilessly on the hillside and the valley till evening came, and evening just as hot and windless. The river ran for miles in that more or less desolate country, covered only on either side with hundreds of acres of great gorse bushes, and here and there a wood or two, all now as dry as tinder and ready to burst into flame at the application of a spark. It reminded Wendover of an old Canadian experience of his, where he had narrowly escaped with his life from a great bush fire, which had destroyed thousands of cattle, and had taken also a large toll of humanity. For on either side of the river these great gorse bushes ran for miles, so that if the wind swept over from the east, and a fire broke out, it would be a terrible thing for any unfortunate human being wandering there with a rod or a gun. But these were only the idle thoughts of an idle man, who fretted and fumed under this enforced inaction, and longed for something to turn up, even though it brought tragedy with it.

And on the seventh day the Rev. James Ogilvy put in an appearance. He came up to the little fishing lodge with his rods and his butterfly net, smiling benignly and gazing about him with that bland air of his, though he certainly started and turned color when he caught sight of Wendover.

"God bless my soul," he exclaimed. "Who on earth would have thought of seeing you here? So you are a friend of the Waltons, are you? I was told that I should find a young man here, but I didn't anticipate the pleasure of meeting Mr. Wendover again. Are you staying here long?"

"That all depends," Wendover said, cautiously. "I came up here, hoping that the rain would come, and, meanwhile, I have done my best with the trout."

"Have you really?" Garcia bleated. "I am afraid that the catching of trout is beyond my poor powers. I hope to catch a salmon for the first time in my life. By the way, what were you doing that afternoon about ten days ago, when you overtook me just outside Brancaster? You see, I changed my mind and drove to Hull instead of waiting for my friend. You were just behind me, I think."

It was all so superbly done and so coolly put that Wendover could not but admire the effrontery of the man.

"Oh, I was just having a run round," he said, carelessly. "And I overtook you on the way. I should probably have gone some distance with you, only I got a bad puncture. I suppose you didn't happen to notice that?"

"Well, I can't say I did," Garcia chuckled. "You see, I'm a pretty bad driver, and all my attention was concentrated on the car. When I looked back you were nowhere to be seen. I hope there was nothing very wrong."

Wendover laughed the matter off. It pleased him to know that this man was not yet sure as to whether Wendover really recognised him or not. But behind Garcia's innocent assumption of almost senile amiability, there was a watching gleam in his eye, and even that disguise of his could not altogether conceal the cruel vindictiveness of his lips. And here lay the great danger. Here was the man whom Wendover had the most cause to fear; here they were together in that lonely spot, miles away from the nearest house, sleeping under the same roof, with only a gilly and an elderly housekeeper as companion. And here would be Garcia's opportunity over and over again. He would accompany Wendover everywhere, he would want to try his hand at trout fishing, of course; they would be alone together in those thousands of acres of gorse, where a hundred crimes might be committed, and no one any the wiser for it. And there were a score of ways by which Garcia could get his enemy at a disadvantage, and so arrange matters to look as if the tragedy had been nothing more than a distressing accident. For they were on high ground there, where here and there the river ran between steep banks, which were miniature precipices in their way, and here and there were deep, silent pools, where a body might lie for weeks without being found. And all this began to get on Wendover's nerves. For two days he had Garcia for his companion, two days when he watched the other's every move and returned in the evening tired and worn out, and almost thankful to find himself alive.

It was on the third day that he slipped away alone, an intensely hot day, with a strong breeze blowing from the north, so that his progress was slow, though this mattered nothing, seeing that he had the whole day before him. He sat down, presently, on a rocky boulder by the side of the stream, and with an uneasy feeling that he was being watched. He told himself that Garcia was getting on his nerves. And, after all, it would be an easy matter for Garcia to follow him and shoot him down, as he had shot down the man with the orange-colored hair. Wendover went back cautiously on his tracks for a quarter of a mile, and dropped into a little hollow behind a thorn bush, where he waited patiently.

He had not long to wait, not more than a quarter of an hour at the outside. And then, as he turned his head, he saw Garcia come creeping along the path that he himself had so recently traversed. The man was stripped of his disguise. He no longer wore the clerical hat or the tinted glasses. He was stripped to his shirt and trousers, and in his right hand Wendover could see the gleam of a revolver. It was Garcia himself who stood there, Garcia, grim and cruel and alert, like some savage animal on the track of his prey. And as he passed the bush, Wendover rose quickly and covered him with his own weapon from which for many weeks he had not been parted, night or day.

"Drop that pistol and put up your hands," he cried. "It is you and I now, John Garcia."

He was looking straight into the eyes of his antagonist. And Garcia seemed to recognise the game was up. Very slowly he raised his hands above his head, and the revolver slipped from his grasp.

"Now, turn your back on me, and walk forward ten paces," Wendover commanded. "After that, don't move an inch, as you value your skin. Come, get a move on."

Garcia obeyed readily enough. He heard his own weapon, as it struck the bushes in the distance, where it was hurled by Wendover, then he turned coolly and deliberately, like a man who knew that his end has come and is prepared to meet it.

"Well," he said quietly. "Well. So you think that you have got the best of John Garcia at last, eh?"

XXV - THE GREATER DANGER

Garcia spoke with all the coolness of a man who is either prepared to meet his fate, or absolutely indifferent to it. He knew that he had overreached himself, and he knew, definitely enough now, that he was face to face with one man who knew his criminal record, and who was ready to put an end to it. The game was up, and well did Garcia know it.

He stood there, in the blazing sunshine, his head bare and the great drops of perspiration standing out on his bald forehead, stood there, grim and cruel like a wolf that is brought to bay, not afraid to die, and ready to take advantage of the first opportunity to escape.

"Well," he said again. "Well? So you know me at last, Mr. Wendover, know me for what I am."

"You may be sure of that," Paul said grimly. "For nearly two years now I have been hard on the track of the blackest-hearted scoundrel in Europe."

"Really! Upon my word, you flatter me. To a certain extent, what you say is a compliment. And may I ask why you have taken all this interest in my welfare?"

"First of all, perhaps, in the general interests of humanity," Paul said. "The man who puts a bullet through your heart is doing a distinct service to society."

"And that you are prepared to do," Garcia sneered.

"I did not say that," Paul replied. "Though I am perfectly prepared to do it if occasion arises. The game is up, Mr. Garcia. It is either you or I, and in the circumstances, I prefer it it to be you. I am not concerned to inquire how you managed to deceive the police at Geneva, because that doesn't very much matter. But I am concerned over the murder of Leo Detmar, the man who helped you to escape. I am concerned in the destruction of de Vince and Petroff, and the assassination of the unfortunate man, Martin. If I wasn't present at those murders, I was very close by and I need not tell you, Mr. Garcia that I know quite enough to have you a dozen times over."

Garcia passed his tongue over his thin lips.

"You are very fortunate," he said. "How fortunate you will perhaps never know. But you have been near to going the way of the rest a hundred times. You are a clever and determined man, and I made the mistake being a little too much afraid of you. I now see that I ought to have removed you first."

"Yes, I think that would have been wiser," Paul said coolly. "But the fact remains that you didn't, and now I hold you powerless at the end of my revolver. We are all alone here, and I am taking no risks. You came here to-day to shoot me, to shoot me in cold blood—"

"You are right there," Garcia admitted.

"To shoot me in cold blood," Paul went on. "And then the coast would have been clear. Once I was out of the way, I take it, that there would have been no life between you and the contents of a certain safe we know of."

Garcia smiled almost pleasantly.

"You are right again," he said. "Why should I try and disguise from a clever man like you what my object has been for the last two years? I am out for money like everybody else, though some people are ashamed to admit it. And after all is said and done, we are all at war with one another where money is concerned. Every man who makes a big fortune ruins a hundred people and perhaps it is more merciful to destroy a rival than allow him to starve. From which you will see I am a bit of a philosopher, Mr. Wendover."

"You are a heartless scoundrel," Paul cried. "You are-but what is that."

Suddenly the wind seemed to increase in velocity. Suddenly it went round to the north-east, and a hotter blast than before struck the two men standing there. Then, all at once, the sun was obscured by drifting clouds of smoke, then with a roar, and a crackle like musketry a great sheet of gorse burst into a wall of flame. It was the spark to inflame the tinder as dry as dust, and it came racing along towards the two men standing there till they could feel the heat on their faces. Then a shower of embers carried across the river, and the fierce devastation thundered out to the other side. It was Wendover who first realised the danger.

"It seems to me," he said coolly, "that neither of us are likely to tell this tale. Mr. Garcia, do you see what has happened? That whole sea of gorse is ablaze and we are in deadly peril. It is useless to cross the river, for the wind has changed and we are trapped. I could shoot you now, without the slightest hesitation, and take my chance of getting away. But it is a slender chance and all we can do is to wait and hope for the best. Now then, are you going to make a confession, or are you not?"

The superb courage of the man did not fail him even at that critical moment. He turned to Paul and faced him as coolly as if they had been at a dinner table.

"For what object?" he asked. "What is there to be gained by it? I have been in a forest fire before, and, though this is a small matter by comparison, it is big enough. We are in the centre of thousands of acres of blazing gorse, and escape is out of the question. I came here to murder you as I murdered the rest, and nature anticipated me. The mere fact that I shall die at the same time is no great consolation, thought it certainly simplifies matters. We shall be choked with cinders and smoke presently. We shall lie down and gasp our lives out side by side; and when the fire has finished with us there will be nothing but a handful of bones to testify to the failure of the great adventure. In ten minutes we shall have a raging furnace behind us, racing along in our direction, at a speed that would outstrip the fastest horse. And if you look you will see that the condition is no better on the other side of the river. The game is up, Mr. Wendover, and it is a case of the devil take the hindmost. And if you ask me if I regret anything, then I don't. I don't even regret that I didn't put a bullet into you months ago. For I have had to take too many chances, and when a man does that sort of thing, fate always plays him a scurvy trick before he has finished. I have felt it from the first in my bones. Something told me that I could never live to possess my treasure. But, on the other hand, you won't have it either. That pleasant little dream of yours of marrying Miss Zena Corroda and living ever afterwards on her money, will not materialise. At any rate, I shall have that consolation to take to another world with me."

The roar of the oncoming flames almost drowned the last few words that Garcia said. And he was not acting now, there was no mistaking the note of sincerity in his voice. With a sudden change of wind, the roar of the flames seemed to jump nearer by miles, and already the thin clouds overhead had obscured the sun and rendered the wood as black as night. Without another word, Garcia dashed forward, and Wendover followed him blindly in the direction of the river. Already it seemed to him that the fierce heat of the day had grown fiercer still. As minute followed minute, the temperature rose till Wendover was conscious of the fact that the perspiration was streaming down his face, and that his limbs were wet as if he had just emerged from his bath. He peeled off his coat and vest, and followed Garcia as best he could.

He was no longer blind to the deadly peril of the advancing flames. He could hear the roar and crackle of them apparently close behind. Already the little tongues of blue and orange danced overhead and jumped from bough to bough, till skyward was a canopy of flame. They could hear the roar of the river presently and the rush of the rapids, but the stream was still afar off, and the going was tangled and dangerous. And still they struggled on side by side as if there were no enmity between them, each man fighting for his life, for there was nothing else at that moment to think of. They were spent and weary now, utterly worn out and exhausted. Already the dropping flames and charred branches were falling on them till their shirts were in rags and the leaping blaze smote them on their bare limbs. Every touch was like a sword-thrust, but they struggled on and on, keeping their feet by a miracle, till at length they stood on the river's bank, looking down a steep bank into the stream forty feet below them.

It was a perilous drop-almost as dangerous as the fire itself. But it had to be done.

"Jump!" Garcia cried, hoarsely. "The only chance."

As he spoke he hurled himself into the air and struck the shallow water with a hideous splash. A second later Paul was after him, blind and almost unconscious. But the cold flood stung him to life again; then, as he rose, he gripped a floating log, and between heaven and earth drifted down the thin stream, heedless and careless as to whether he lived or died.

XXVI - THE TREASURE

Wendover was back in London again, puzzled and uneasy in his mind. Even now he did not know whether he had failed or not. He himself had been dragged out of the shallow stream, where he had lain, half-suffocated for hours, by a friendly charcoal-burner, who had found him there, more dead than alive, and had taken him up to the shooting box where, for a day or two, he had been quite unable to give any account of his adventures. Then he had deemed it prudent to tell his friends that Garcia had been in his company, but he said no more, and as Garcia had not put in an appearance, and the most careful inquiries failed to elicit any information about him, it was naturally assumed that he had perished in the flames. The odds were largely in favor of his having done so.

But, then, Garcia was no ordinary man: he had looked death in the face too often to be taken by surprise, and possibly he had taken advantage of a stroke of good fortune to disappear altogether for the time being.

If this was so-and it was clearly possible-he would assuredly crop up somewhere else in a fresh disguise and strike Wendover down at the moment when he felt most safe. There was nothing for it, then, but to wait for the few weeks which would elapse between now and the annual meeting of the Brotherhood. If Garcia were alive he would most assuredly put in an appearance on that occasion. He would take it for granted the last of his foes was out of the way, and that the treasure in the safe was waiting for him without the slightest chance of any other claimant putting in an appearance. So Paul went down south and nursed himself carefully with a view to what might turn out to be the final round between Garcia and himself.

Zena was not in London, she was still down on the south coast completing her holiday. She was staying in rooms there, and at the end of a week or so Wendover ran down to see her. He was still pale and shaky, but his eyes shone clearly enough, and his nerves had recovered their tension. Still, Zena was shocked at the change in his appearance, and the tears came into her eyes, as she hung about her lover's neck and implored him not to carry the adventure any further.

"Why should you go on, Paul?" she urged. "Let that wretch have the money, if he is still alive. There seems to be a sort of curse upon it. I don't think I could ever touch it myself after what has happened."

"You mustn't blame the money itself," Paul said. "Money is an insensate thing, and if everybody who possessed a fortune really deserved it, there would be little wealth in the world. Besides, think what a powerful instrument of evil to put in Garcia's hands. No, my dear girl, that money belongs to you, and I have sworn by all my gods that I will recover it. I shall take every precaution. I shall not go to the rendezvous unarmed, and if Garcia has the temerity to meet me there, then, by heaven, he shall pay the penalty."

"But suppose you don't go?" Zena urged. "Suppose you stay away for another year. Surely we can wait that time. And then it would be safe."

"And have the suspense hanging over my head all that time." Paul said. "Oh, no. We shall be married long before then, Zena, and even if it is only for your sake, I must convince myself that Garcia is dead. If he fails to turn up next week, we shall know that that man exists no longer. So, if you don't mind, let's forget all about him and make the best of the happy week that lies before us. I want to see that haunted look fade from your eyes. I want to see the bloom on your cheeks again, and the laughter on your lips. Come, let us get out in the sunshine, let us go and see happy people enjoying themselves, heedless of the fact that such creatures as Garcia exist."

On the morning of the meeting of the Brotherhood Wendover turned his back on the little watering-place and made his way to London by an early train. He wanted to be alone now, he wanted to concentrate himself upon the task before him, and, above all, he wanted to forget the keen anxiety in Zena's dark eyes as she parted from him at the station. She had been anxious to accompany him to London, so that she might be on the spot to hear the news at the first available moment, but Paul had been absolutely firm on that point. He wanted nothing to hamper him now, he wanted to get the work over and done with, and then he would join Zena at Sandmouth on the morrow by the earliest possible train. And he was feeling rather more anxious than he was prepared to admit, for the long strain had told upon him.

The slow day dragged its way along till evening came at length, and Paul turned his face in the direction of his destination. He tried to argue with himself; he tried to persuade himself that there was no real danger, but, all the same, he was feeling exceedingly anxious and nervous. He dined at a quiet restaurant, and forced himself to sit out a frivolous musical comedy afterwards. It was only when he turned into the noisy street, just after eleven, that he realised the fact that the performance had been entirely a blank to him, and, indeed, he had not the haziest idea what the play was about. Then, with something like a sigh of relief, he turned into the vestibule of the Ambassadors' Hotel at a quarter to twelve. As the clock was striking the hour, he strolled leisurely along the corridor, and stood outside the door of the fateful room with the latchkey in his hand. Then, with his courage all back again in him, and his teeth closely set, he pushed back the lock and stepped into the anteroom. The inner door was ajar, and he looked cautiously in.

The supper-room was empty!

The clock had struck twelve, and the last ringing chime had died away as Wendover took stock of his surroundings. If Garcia had been coming, then assuredly he would have been here before now. For the combination on the time lock had undoubtedly worked, and it was open to anyone to pull back that heavy door and help themselves to the treasure. But no one was here, there was no sound in the corridor outside, and apparently no one was coming. Paul stepped forward.

The cold repast was on the table, the gold-foiled bottles stood on the sideboard, and, best of all, the iron door of the safe had swung open. Paul's first impulse, in this moment of suspense — a suspense that brought the beads of moisture out on his forehead-was to clear out the contents of the safe and fly before the dread interruption came.

But Paul fought the feeling down valiantly. It was in his own hands, now, to know, once and for all, whether the future was clear and tranquil, and any sudden impulse on his part might have prolonged the uncertainty, perhaps for years to come. He sat there, doggedly, watching the clock tick off minute after minute till the first and second and third quarter were passed, and from somewhere in the distance a big knell. Then, with a wild joy in his heart, and a feeling of relief that brought a lump in his throat, he turned to the safe and began to fill his pockets.

There was practically no gold there, nothing but piles of bank notes and negotiable securities, and some papers that Wendover dropped, and with a lighted match, burned to ashes. On the top of these he placed his mask, and then, holding himself with an effort, closed the safe and left the room.

A moment or two later he was in the street, wiping the moisture from his forehead, and trying to realise that Garcia was dead, and that many years of happiness and prosperity for Zena and himself lay snugly in the depths of his overcoat pocket. For he had won out beyond the shadow of a doubt. Pluck and courage, and patience had carried him through, and for the rest, the great adventure was finished.

A glorious sunshine lay over the little sheltered cove at Sandmouth, where Zena sat alone, waiting for the coming of her lover. He had not kept her in suspense, for an hour or two ago, she had had a telegram from Wendover, which in a few words told her everything. She knew now that she had come into her own, she knew that the treasure was safe in Wendover's bank, and that the shadow of peril had vanished for ever. It had been a long and dangerous adventure for Wendover, but it was over at last, and a higher power than man had avenged the lives of the men that Garcia had so recklessly destroyed. Small wonder, then, that the light of happiness gleamed in Zena's dark eyes and that the radiant smile on her face deepened as she looked up and saw the man who had gone through so much for her, coming eagerly down the path leading from the cliffs. And a moment later she was in Wendover's arms.

It was a long time before either of them spoke, a long time before either of them cared to break the delicious silence of that blissful moment. Then Wendover told Zena everything.

"It has been a black and bitter time," he said. "But it is all over now. You can enjoy the fortune which is rightly yours without fear and without reproach."

"I shall enjoy it all the more," Zena said, "because I know that you are going to share it with me. But for you, Paul, I should still be struggling for my daily bread. What a wonderful contrast between now and this time last year, between this time and last night. And, Paul, I want you to make a promise. I want you to have no more adventures. I want a nice house in the country, where you can have your sport like other men. I want to rest and be happy."

"Anything I can give you!" Paul cried.

"You have given me all I need already," Zena whispered. "Never was a girl yet who had a hero as good and true and brave as mine."

THE END

www.ingramcontent.com/pod-product-compliance
Ingram Content Group UK Ltd.
Pitfield, Milton Keynes, MK11 3LW, UK
UKHW021924190726
13853UKWH00002B/825

9 788027 336562